WHISPERING SECRETS

Joe Tamillo

Joseph Tamillo

Whispering Secrets

Copyright © 2009 Joseph Tamillo. All rights reserved. No part of this book may be reproduced or retransmitted in any form or by any means without the written permission of the publisher.

Published by Wheatmark®
610 East Delano Street, Suite 104, Tucson, Arizona 85705
U.S.A.
www.wheatmark.com

ISBN: 978-1-60494-216-3
LCCN: 2008941638

Acknowledgments

Two priests—Fathers John Mitchell and Mike Krenik—helped me with much of the religious data used in my novel. They deserve special thanks.

I wish to thank Scott Le Doux, former heavyweight prize fighter from Minnesota, for his assistance with boxing technique.

I am especially grateful to all of my high school and college English teachers who made the study of literature and writing important in my life.

Many thanks go to my friends who have encouraged me to write and have critiqued my writings. A number of my closest friends, some of whom are now deceased, appear as characters.

Bob Vernon, my former student and athlete, created the memorable sketches that give life and meaning to all of my characters. His drawings on the front and back covers also credit his genius.

Finally, Chuck Dolinar, a friend and former teaching colleague, deserves credit for editing my manuscript, and Kirk Lindberg, his son-in-law, for providing technical assistance.

Introduction

The creation of this novel spans almost sixty years of my life. The original thought of writing this novel came during my high school days. By the time I graduated from Duke University in 1952, I had written the first part of the story, but my heavy involvement in teaching, coaching, and raising a family prevented me from completing it until now.

The references in this story to altar boys, church, priests, the gym, carnival life, and the Golden Glove tournament are somewhat autobiographical, but the majority of this novel is fictional.

I attended a Catholic high school in Duluth, Minnesota. While living there, I worked out at a local gym, participated in boxing, and competed in a Golden Glove tournament.

My aunt and uncle owned a carnival in St. Louis,

Missouri, and for three summers, I went to Missouri to work with the carnival.

In the fall of 1945 my parents gave their permission, and I joined the U.S. Marine Corps, serving for four years. Upon completion of boot camp, I was sent to Guam, Japan, and China. While overseas, I wrote many poems and articles dealing with my experiences in those countries.

In 1949 I played football for the Quantico Marine football team. As a result of playing Marine football, I received numerous college scholarship offers, and I decided to play for Duke University.

It was at Duke that I became interested in becoming an English teacher. One of my courses was American Literature, and it was in this course that I was asked to write a term paper about an American novelist. I chose Ernest Hemingway. His individuality was what caught my attention, especially his interest in prize fighting. Shortly after writing that term paper, I gave thought to writing either an autobiographical sketch or to embark on writing a novel.

Upon graduating from Duke University in 1952, I became a public school English instructor, and I taught for over thirty-five years. During this teaching career, I wrote two books of personal poems: *Our Asian Experience*, 1985, and *See What I Saw*. My teaching career prompted me to write many articles and short stories.

I ended my high school teaching career at White Bear Senior High School in White Bear Lake, Minnesota, when I retired in May, 1985.

INTRODUCTION

I am now eighty years old. After nearly sixty years of intermittent writing, this novel is now complete.

Contents

1. On the Way to St. Jude 1
2. Wednesday Night Fights 9
3. Dean's Past Experiences 14
4. Father Dillon's Dream 21
5. A Busy Schedule 24
6. In Father's Footsteps 28
7. Sluice – the Second Meeting 34
8. Sam's Bar 37
9. Max's Gym 42
10. The New Altar Boy 46
11. Two Life Changing Events 50
12. Father's Boxing Career 55
13. A Serious Workout 59
14. A New Manager 67

15.	The First Fight	74
16.	Jose Zapata	82
17.	Max's Boxing Career	98
18.	A Formidable Foe	104
19.	A Non-Title Fight	115
20.	Fight Night	140
21.	A Great Opportunity	150
22.	The Preparation	158
23.	The Championship Bout	165
24.	Future Plans	175

One

On the Way to St. Jude

Dean rubbed his eyes and moved to the side of his bed. He glanced quickly at the alarm clock near by. It was close to 6:00 a.m. He would eat a bowl of cereal and be on his way to Chicago. He had just enough money to pay for his rented room and a little left for food along the way. He couldn't afford a bus ticket, so he would have to depend on hitching rides along the way, but he also realized that Chicago was miles away. He sat thinking of his present situation. He did not have full employment, and the jobs he was able to get hardly paid enough for his rent. He thought about relatives, but how many of them would want to care for a nineteen year old young man. He had stopped thinking of going back to his home now that his parents were divorced. He felt that neither his dad nor mother really understood him. As for his one older brother, he was in the service and Dean didn't even know where he was stationed. Since dropping out of school in the tenth grade, and with no high school diploma, few companies would even employ him. No, Dean had to count on this trip to Chicago. He had visited his parish priest, and his priest told him all about a certain Father Dillon. He was told that Father Dillon took in homeless youngsters and that he provided them with food and lodging until the youngsters were able to find suitable employment which would pay for their room and board and limited spending. Father Dillon was well known for these endeavors. Dean, however, knew very little about Father Dillon or his church, St. Jude. He would have to trust his parish priest and at least make the journey to Chicago.

Dean poured the remaining milk onto his breakfast cereal. He dressed and put a few items into a small back pack. He didn't want to be burdened with anything large and bulky. He had not done much hitch hiking, so this would be another growing experience. He put his rent into a small envelope along with a short note explaining briefly his plans to hitch rides to Chicago and then to St. Jude. He didn't want his landlord to send the police after him. Dean was ready to take another step to find a meaningful job and a meaningful life. Maybe St. Jude and Father Dillon could help to resolve his many problems.

"Just fifty more miles," whispered Dean, "and hopefully I'll find this Father Dillon and possibly get a new start." It was getting dark, and Dean realized that he had only minutes left if he hoped to hitch another ride. Having to walk fifty or more miles didn't especially interest him. Even though he was on a major highway, the traffic at dusk was sparse. Off in the distance, Dean saw the piercing lights of an oncoming vehicle, and he walked to the road shoulder with his hand outstretched and his thumb pointing in a forward motion. The car sped by as if the occupants had not seen him on the roadside, but almost as fast as the car had passed him, Dean realized that it had come to an immediate halt.

In fact, the car was in reverse and closing the gap rapidly. "What a break," was all that Dean could say. He noticed that there were three teenage boys in the car, but because of the oncoming darkness, he was unable to see their faces. He heard clearly one of the boys ask where he was going and if he wanted to go with them.

"I'm headed for St. Jude's Church to meet a Father Dillon," Dean replied. The teen in the back seat moved over to the other side. The other teen got out of the passenger front seat and opened the back door.

"Climb in," he said, and Dean hurriedly got into the back seat as the car lurched forward. For some reason, Dean instantly had a strange feeling about this ride. He had received rides before, but he had never even thought about any dangers when hitching rides. One of the teens said, "Sluice, why did we stop for this punk?"

"Shut up," was the quick reply, followed by, "What's your name, kid?"

"I'm Dean Nelson. I was told that I might get a week or two lodging at Father Dillon's place."

"If you ever get to Father Dillon's, he will definitely give you immediate lodging," barked the teen driver, "but you'll have to get to Father Dillon's place."

Dean caught the meaning of those words instantly. He realized that before this ride was over, he would pay a big price. Dean straightened his back and waited. The car speeded up, going miles over the regular speed limit. A half hour passed and nothing more was said by anyone. Dean could see the lights of the approaching city as the car veered off the highway onto a dirt road.

"Get out," yelled the teen driver. Dean opened the back door and stepped from the vehicle. As he did this, he heard the front doors open and then slam shut. Was this to be his greeting to Father Dillon's home and parish? With the lights of the car off, he was surrounded by the darkness. One of the teens jumped on Dean's back, and Dean found himself on the ground, unable to protect himself. He felt the thud of heavy shoes pound into his back and legs. If he could only get to his feet, he might have a chance to defend himself. He rolled over and tried desperately to get to his feet. As he up righted himself, a fist smashed into his face, and Dean felt the ground again.

"Come on, let's get out of here. We've already left our calling card, so he won't stay in this area very long." Those were the last words that Dean heard as he slipped into an unconscious state.

Dean's eyes opened ever so slowly. He was in a ditch beside the dirt road. He remembered the attack by the three teens. His back and legs ached like he had never before experienced. Something caused him to wipe off his mouth, and dried blood plus fresh blood appeared on his hand. He remembered the smash to his face and that was all.

Dean slowly got to his knees and pushed himself upward so that he was in a standing position. He widened his feet to give him added balance. The very fact that he could move his legs indicated that he might still be able to walk back to the main highway and that he might be able to pursue his designed course. The town could only be a few miles away. He put his hands into his pockets and much to his surprise, the few dollars were still there. The teens obviously had no plans to rob him, but what could be their reason for giving him such a beating? He pondered the situation; he would remember the one name, Sluice, that he had heard. Should they meet again, Dean would be prepared to defend himself.

Dean dusted off his clothing and walked painfully to the highway. He would be more careful when hitching his next ride. It wasn't long before a pickup truck with an older man driving pulled over to where he stood. The driver took a quick glance at Dean.

"You've been in a fight, boy—where are you headed?"

Dean sensed that he could trust this old man. He opened the passenger side door and climbed in.

"That's quite a cut on your lip, son. You should have some stitches put in it."

"I wish I could," was Dean's reply, "but I have very little money. And besides, I have no way of finding a clinic, let alone an emergency hospital."

"Don't worry, my boy, I know Dr. Browman. He will stitch up that cut, and I'll take care of the charges. He owes me for some odd jobs that I did for him recently, so I'm not worried about his fees—and you needn't worry either. What brings you to these parts?"

"I was told that a Father Dillon sometimes helps guys like me. I'd be willing to work to pay my way, but right now I'm downright broke."

"Father Dillon, you say? You couldn't find a better person to help you get back on your feet. Father Dillon is something special in these parts. He may be just about the best known person in the county."

The old man started his pickup and drove in the direction of the city.

"By the way," Dean asked, "what's your name?"

"My name is Jeb Stuart. I'm a retired farmer, but I still have my home and a few acres of land for gardening. Don't make much more than I get from my social security checks, but I earn a few bucks doing side jobs like the ones I did for Browman. I get by, and that's about all I really need. My wife, Martha, passed away a few years back. Much of my family is spread across the country, so I'm pretty much alone. My dog Kirby, a golden retriever, always barks and licks my face, so I do have some company. When I get too down in the dumps, I drive over to Father Dillon's place. He always has fresh coffee, donuts or sandwiches, and we shoot the bull and pass away the time. Father Dillon always seems to build up my spirits, so when I leave his place, I usually feel a hundred times better. I'm certain that he will treat you much the same way. He'll be a true friend if you are looking for a friend."

Jeb leaned back in his truck. It wasn't too long before he was pulling into the driveway of Dr. Browman. Dean saw the sign, "Dr. Jay Browman, Physician."

Jeb got out of the truck and knocked on the front door. The door opened and Jeb stepped in. It wasn't but a few minutes before Jeb opened the door and motioned for Dean to come in. Dr. Browman pointed Dean to a special chair.

"That's quite a cut, son," was Dr. Browman's first comment. "You get into a fight or something? It's none of my business, but with a few teen gangs roaming the streets at night, I get my share of beaten teens. I always ask if they know who hit them, but I seldom get any responses. Fear has a funny way of clamming up these swollen faces."

With that, Dr. Browman had finished stitching up Dean's lip.

"Take these pills so that you don't get any infection.

You'll be okay in a few days. Might have a little trouble eating, but that lip should heal rapidly."

Jeb thanked his friend, and Dean and Jeb turned toward the truck.

Dean thanked the doctor. "I'm going to Father Dillon's for a week or so. If I get any paying jobs, I'll be back to pay you for your services." Dr. Browman smiled and shut the door.

Dean thought quietly to himself that not all was bad in the world around him. Jeb was one person that Dean would long remember, and Dr. Browman held a special place in Dean's mind.

"I told you that you wouldn't have anything to worry about in seeing Doc. There are some really fine people in this city, and you are about to meet a very special person, Father Dillon."

With these words, Jeb turned into another driveway. Dean noticed the white picket fence and the small church that neighbored Father Dillon's home. He had arrived. Jeb said that he had some other things to do, so he simply instructed Dean to knock on the screened front door. Wouldn't be too long and it would be darkened night again, but Dean knew that the next evening wouldn't repeat what he had just gone through. Dean heard Jeb yell, "Wednesday night is Father Dillon's fight night. If he seems a bit cranky when you walk in, just disregard him. He watches the Wednesday night fights every week, and he doesn't like to be disturbed. Everyone in his parish knows better than to bother him on his special night." Jeb started his truck and drove away.

Two

Wednesday Night Fights

"**IN THIS CORNER** weighing one hundred and sixty pounds and wearing purple trunks, the middle weight champion of the world...." The Wednesday night fights were on the air, and Father Dillon wasn't about to miss this fight. The announcer continued his introduction of both fighters. Only the light of the TV tube illuminated the room. To the visible eye the room appeared empty, but a wisp of smoke rose to mingle with the rays of the TV's light. Except for the TV, there was no other light in the room. An old fashioned padded arm chair centered the room. Some two feet in front of the chair was a modernistic foot stool. The other furnishings, a studio-couch, a desk and straight back chair, were an assortment of modern, colonial, and transitional styles. It was quite evident that either the furnishings were gifts of parishioners, or the old priest had no eye for furniture. It was the housekeeper's night off.

Wednesday was always her night off. Some ham sandwiches on rye and iced tea stood on a tray near the padded chair.

The bell sounded the beginning of the first round. This was the fight that Father Dillon had waited for a long time. He knew the fight game. In fact, there were times when his parishioners felt that he had more interest in the fights than in saving souls. Father Dillon might have argued this point on any given Sunday, but he wouldn't argue religion or soul savings on a Wednesday night.

The first round was typical of most fights. It was slow and deliberate. Both fighters sensed the importance of this fight, and they were content to feel each other out. Father Dillon pushed further into his chair, reached for one of the sandwiches, and fixed his gaze on the tube. The bell sounded the second round. The second was much like the first, but in the third round the champion's left hand landed squarely. The count began. One, two, three....

"Get up! This might be your only chance at the championship. Don't you understand? You have a chance to be the middle weight champion of the world..."

The priest sat on the edge of his chair. For the first time his face was discernible. A first glimpse revealed a rather fleshy nose. Thin lined lips indicated that this man was no longer a participant. His ring experience had become that of an ardent spectator. A closely cut crew cut made Father Dillon look more athletic, and it accented his youthful interests. The stooped over position made it impossible to discern his other physical features.

Slowly the challenger got to one knee.

"You can make it...."

The bell sounded. The challenger's handlers jumped into the ring. Almost instinctively they worked to revive their fighter. The bell signaled round four. The champion was like a leopard stalking his prey. It was only a matter of time. Father Dillon had seen this same scene hundreds of times. He remembered the home town gym, the 20 ounce gloves his father gave him, the golden glove eliminations, the long grueling hours of training, the newspaper clippings, the first professional fight, ambition....

The door buzzer broke the train of Father Dillon's thoughts. At first there was no movement from the chair. The buzzer sounded again, this time a little longer.

"The challenger lands a solid left hand......"

Now who in the world is that? This is my night. How many times have I told them not to interrupt me on Wednesday night? Father O'Brien's a baseball fan, and there's no game tonight. Why don't they bother him?

"Oh, all right, I'm coming." Father Dillon pushed his small but well built body into an upright position. His eyes were still on the TV as he trod his way to the door. His hand snapped a switch as if by rote. A quick thrust of the left hand, and he pushed open the door.

In a voice other than cordial he asked, "Well, what do you want? Don't you know what night this is? Well, don't just stare, say something." Father Dillon fired question after question. The intruder stood in a state of shock. "Well, if you're not going to say anything, at least come in. You can walk, can't you?"

The tall lanky boy in his teens followed his handler into the TV-lit room. The priest resumed his vigil at the screen. "What a come back! The challenger hit the champ with every combination in the book. He forced the champ to hang on during the closing seconds of the fifth round," blurted the announcer just before round six began.

"You see what you did? You caused me to miss probably the best round of the fight. "

"You a fight fan, Father?" murmured the newcomer in a shaky voice. If Father Dillon heard the few words, he made no attempt to respond. He continued watching the set. By the end of the eighth round, Father saw what few fans would ever see or ever understand. The challenger, a. known boxer, came flatfooted to the middle of the ring at the start of the ninth round. A boxer, if he plans to win, must move, hit, jab, and move some more. The puncher stalks his opponent. Both of his feet are planted to give him that added strength, but here was the boxer, flatfooted. Father knew the challenger was tiring.

"Whom are you pulling for?" said a somewhat stronger voice. At first, the priest disregarded the comment of his young visitor, but he reconsidered and replied.

"Why, the challenger, of course!" knowing quite well that the challenger would not be the winner.

"He doesn't have a chance. His legs are giving out. He'll be lucky to finish the tenth." Father Dillon could see that the boy was staring at him when he made his remarks.

"I suppose you knew a fighter, or maybe you went to a Catholic school. Used to be all Catholic high schools had boxing as one of their sports?"

"No, I had a few fights, nothing really big, but I got the feel of the ring and when I got tired, I could always feel it in my legs. They just seemed to give out."

By this time Father Dillon was listening attentively to the boy. He had even taken his eyes off the picture box.

"You know something, boy, you're right on target. His legs are gone."

Almost as if he had called the round, the challenger took three straight right hands; he staggered near the ropes. It was all over. Father Dillon lifted his person from the chair, flicked the dial to off, and turned the living room lights on.

Three

Dean's Past Experiences

"I SUPPOSE YOU'RE hungry? How about ham on rye? The iced tea must be diluted by now, but you're welcome to it."

"Thanks a lot! Nothing I like better than ham sandwiches." The boy moved toward the tray. The priest refilled his pipe, lit it, and returned to his former position. He eyed the boy rather carefully, noticing that the boy had brought no luggage with him. As far as he could see, the boy's sole belongings were on his physical person.

Father Dillon opened the conversation. "Well, son, what can I do for you? It's quite obvious that you didn't come here to watch the fights. I guess you did try to communicate with me during the fight, but that's another subject. Live in this area? What's your name? What brings you here?" Father Dillon finished his last interrogatory sentence. But he was like that. He was always asking questions and talking. He wasn't one to listen, but he was offering the boy a chance to speak, and so Dean began.

"My name is Dean Nelson. I'm nineteen. Sort of a high school dropout. I attended a Catholic high school. About the only things that I really liked were sports. I was on the boxing squad and played guard in football. I was one of the few freshmen on the varsity team. I quit after finishing the tenth grade. When I was twelve, my mother sent me to help her sister, Harriet, who owned a carnival in St. Louis, Missouri. Each summer that I went to Missouri was a real learning experience. A Bob Fitzimmons always selected me to be part of his crew. I was part of the crews that put up the merry-go-round. He taught me a lot about life and its challenges. In fact, I considered him a second father. Since Bob couldn't eat in the local cafes, I would get our food and we would sit together eating. I once asked him if he liked chicken and watermelon. He turned the question immediately around and asked me if I liked them. When I said I did, he just beamed a big smile. At the time, I didn't fully understand his reply, but I certainly do now. Met some interesting people who worked for my aunt and uncle, two of whom I won't forget. One was named Sleepy. I guess he got that name because he didn't work too fast, and he was always napping when we didn't have work to do. Blackie was another one. I had never seen anyone with such big muscles. He was a bull of a man, but he was also a dangerous man. He once accused me of telling my uncle that he and some of the other workers were keeping the ride money. I never ever told my uncle anything about the crew members, but I knew Blackie didn't believe me. Once I was working on the Ferris wheel towers, and we were pulling the metal spokes of the wheel into place. I had one foot on the tower and my other foot on one of the steel girders on the spoke. Blackie let the pull-up rope drop, and I almost fell from the top of the wheel. I didn't care to work with Blackie, but after that incident, I let him know that I wouldn't sleep lightly if I were Blackie. He seemed to get what I was talking about, and he left me alone after that.

"We played many small towns and churches, so I got to see a lot of Missouri, but getting back to Bob, he was like Uncle Remus, always smiling and never ever complaining. I learned a lot about humility from that man. Shortly after dropping out of school, I got a few small jobs as an errand boy, gas station attendant, and usher in one of the big city's theaters. My folks were divorced. My old man lives somewhere in Minneapolis, and my mother— Father Dillon noticed that the boy referred to his mom as mother—she's remarried. I guess the guy she married has two children. That would sort of make me an outsider. I never really liked her second husband anyway. I've got an older brother who's in the Marines. We don't write, so he doesn't know where I am. I hiked to Chicago. Funny how Carl Sandburg writes of Chicago as if it were a king's palace. I remember reading some of his poetry just before I quit school. I still can't see all of the beauty that he speaks of, but I guess I can't see much beauty in anything anymore. When you lose your parents and get pushed into the world the way I have, you start feeling sorry for yourself and, brother, that's when it really gets to you."

"Where did you learn about boxing?"

"'Like I told you, Father, I went to a Catholic school, and boxing was one of the sports offered. We mostly fought opponents from other Catholic schools, because few of the local public high schools had boxing. I got into boxing by chance. I haven't read too many books in my life, but I did read about Hemingway's life, about how he likes hunting and boxing. Since I didn't make friends very easily, I got to enjoy the individuality that boxing offered. If I made a mistake, it would be my fault; I would control my own destiny."

Father Dillon was smiling. He thought this could be what he had been waiting for. "How many fights did you have?"

"Probably a dozen or so," was Dean's reply. "Fought as a welterweight. Though I didn't have a lot of ring experiences, I did work out a lot at a local gym. The owner was a former fighter. When he had extra time, and when he wasn't working with some of the other fighters, he would work with me. He taught me a lot of things: how to use the speed bag, the heavy punching bag, the jumping ropes, the weights, and just about everything else he had in his small gym. A lot of the times, I would just shadow box in front of the many mirrors which walled his gym. He was in my corner when I fought in a local golden glove tournament. I fought three fights in that tournament, but I lost in the semi-finals. The guy that beat me went on to the finals in Detroit. I learned fast that there is always someone bigger and better than you in the ring. Though I've never been knocked out, I was knocked down three times when I lost in the golden glove semi-finals. The gym's owner really reamed me out after that fight. He told me that each time I got knocked down, I was pulling straight back after throwing my right hand. Never, never go straight back. You leave yourself an open target for a straight left or right. I've never forgotten those comments, and I have never been knocked down since. I didn't like picking myself off the canvas. Well, Father, that about sums up my short life and my brief boxing career."

Father Dillon had noticed Dean's swollen lip. "Looks as if you've had your own fight this evening. That's a bad looking lip. What happened?"

At first Dean was reluctant to tell the old priest about his earlier encounter, but since he also didn't want to lie, he explained, "I was on the highway hitch hiking with the hope of finding someone who might be able to direct me to your church. This car pulled over. Three teens asked me to climb in. Without really thinking about anything but finding your place, I climbed into the back seat of the car. It wasn't minutes and I realized that I shouldn't have been so quick to get into their car. One of the teens said, 'Sluice, why did we stop for this punk?' 'Shut up,' was the quick reply. The driver asked me where I was going, and I told him that I was looking for a Father Dillon who would give me lodging for a week or two. He asked me my name, and I told him, 'Dean Nelson.'

"The driver responded, 'If you ever get to Father Dillon's, he'll definitely give you food and lodging, but that's if you get to his place.' I knew at that moment the mistake I had made by climbing into their car. The driver drove at breakneck speed. He finally pulled off the main road onto a dirt road and stopped. 'Get out,' the driver said. It was quite dark by then, so I had trouble seeing their faces. I think you can figure out what happened after that. The worst part of the whole ordeal was that I had no chance to defend myself. When I righted myself after being knocked to the ground, a fist to my face caused me to black out. Fortunately for me, they didn't feel it necessary to hit me again. When I awoke, I was in a ditch by the side of a dirt road. I managed to get to my feet. I knew I had been cut because I felt moist blood on my lips. Somehow or other, I got back to the main highway. It wasn't too long before an old truck pulled up to me. He took a quick look at me, and he realized that I had been in a fight.

"'Climb in, son,' he said, and then asked where I was headed, but he also said that I should first tend to my lip. I told him that I didn't have the money for a doctor.

"'Don't worry, son,' said the old man, 'I know a Dr. Browman who owes me some favors. He'll stitch up your lip, give you a few pills, and you will be as good as new.'

"'By the way,' I said, 'what's your name?' 'Jeb Stuart,' was the reply. The doc knew about the roving gangs in the area. He had treated similar patients. He stitched up my lip and gave me some pills to take to ward off an infection. I thanked the Doc and told him that I was hoping to find a certain priest, a Father Dillon. I also told the Doc that I would be back to pay him. He thanked me, shook Jeb's hand, and Jeb and I were off to your place. You know the rest of the story."

Father Dillon looked squarely at Dean and said, "You will want to stay far away from Sluice and his bunch. They're no good. There was a day when Sluice and his followers played on the church's playground, but now that they are a few years older, it's the drugs, smokes, and beatings which they enjoy. You will meet Sluice again if you ever decide to walk with me on my daily visits to various places and people."

Four

Father Dillon's Dream

FATHER DILLON CONTINUED to stare at the boy, almost as if he hadn't heard a single spoken word. "A fighter, huh? A bed for the night? A job? Funny, but I was thinking of hiring a young lad. I'm not as young as I used to be. There are a lot of things I can't do anymore. The more I think about it, I could use a boy like you. I can't pay you too much, but I can guarantee you three meals and your own room. What's more, I can introduce you to a few store keepers who'll give you odd jobs. You might be able to earn a little more that way."

"Oh, that's all right, Father. I just want enough to get by. I can't promise you that I'll stay over a month. If I find what I'm looking for, I'll give you advanced notice of my intentions."

"Let's cut the talk for tonight. I'll bet you'd like to shower and get to bed. Follow me. I'll show you your room. Since you mentioned that you might not stay on with me, I may as well tell you that your room has housed many different types of boys. Some spent one night, and Larry, would you believe it, spent seven months. If only he had been willing to work harder, he could have made it." The old priest was thinking out loud.

"Could have made what?"

Father Dillon shrugged his shoulders. "Oh, I was just thinking out loud. Forget it." He pushed open the door to the small copy room. "You'll find a towel and soap in the cabinet in the bathroom. I'll see you in the morning. Want to get up for 6:00 o'clock Mass?"

Dean managed to utter weakly, "No, I haven't been to church in a long time. I don't mean to offend you, Father, but I really haven't had much time for God either. Maybe some other time." The door closed behind the boy.

Father Dillon walked to his own room. Preparing for bed, he thought of two things that had taken place that night. A young boy, a boxer, had come into his employment; one that had lost sight of God. Was it a coincidence or not? His life had been spent in helping others to find God, but now he was confronted with another side of his life that he had kept hidden for all of these years. Father Dillon was well known for his interest in athletic endeavors, but few, if any, knew that he, as a young boy, had aspirations to be a boxing champion. His interest in the Wednesday night fights was more then just a passing interest. He was reliving and yes, still living the actions, the frustrations that each fighter felt as he climbed into the ring. Father Dillon, externally and internally, was a devoted priest, but he had had another ambition. He saw in Dean a chance to realize that ambition. Why not? He said he had had a few fights.

He didn't say anything about not liking to fight. He's got the physique of a fighter, and unless I miss my guess, he has the temperament to be a good one. In the darkness of his room, Father Dillon knelt by his bed. The prayer he said was unlike any he had previously said. "Please, dear Lord, guide me in the handling of this young boy. If it be Your wish that Dean be a prizefighter, give me the strength of my convictions to guide him. Amen." The devout priest pulled back the covers of his bed and climbed into it. As he lay peering into the darkness, a confident smile crossed his lips. He closed his eyes and slept.

FATHER DILLON WALKED up the two steps to the altar. He lifted his face to God and began saying the Mass. A few women, heads covered discreetly, knelt in the pew, but Father Dillon's success as God's servant could hardly be judged by the numbers now in his little church. He lifted the chalice. As he looked out into the vacant little church, he noticed a young boy sitting in the last row. It was Dean. '"Thank you, God," whispered the priest. The first step had been taken. At that moment he knew that his prayers would be answered.

Five

A Busy Schedule

"**Mary, meet Dean** Nelson." Mary was Father Dillon's capable housekeeper. She had been with him for some twenty years. Mary eyed Dean as if she were giving her approval or disapproval of his presence. "He may be with us for a little while. I've given him a job, so if you have anything around the house for him to do, speak out." At this comment, Mary turned and smiled at Father Dillon.

"Is this another of your lost souls to save, Father?" With that said, she turned to Dean. "Welcome, lad. Another hand around here can always be useful. There are a number of things in the basement that should be cleaned and moved. We can start down there, but how about breakfast first. How do you like your eggs?"

"Oh, I'm not particularly fussy. It's been a long time since I had what I would call a real breakfast." Mary placed two sunny side eggs, some fries, and a slice of ham on his plate. She filled his glass with orange juice. Father's plate looked much the same.

"In the name of the Father, and of the Son..." Father Dillon blessed himself and said a short prayer before touching his food. Dean's mouth was already filled, but he did sense the situation, and so he slowly bowed his head. After all, a boy without a family can hardly be expected to remember grace.

"I suppose you're going to follow your routine for the day?" questioned Mary. Monday, like most days in the week was Father's busiest day. He had to cover a large area, which included a visit to the hospital and the sick, the local jail, the YMCA—yes, Father Dillon frequented that place. He could get to see the facilities for recreation, the pool, and the dedicated workers. They were doing a job for the youth, a job which had to be done in this neighborhood. His day would carry him past some of the local bars. Day or night, these were frequented by some of the lost souls. For some reason or other, these lost souls looked for Father Dillon. He would counsel many of them. Oh, he didn't convert many, but they learned to respect what he was trying to accomplish, and for this wise priest it was a good start. There were even times when he would sit at the bar with a glass of beer in his hand. This might not be the customary way to preach God's word, but it had impact.

Invariably Father would frequent the shabby playgrounds which seemed to lose their identities with the many apartment dwellings around them.

The playgrounds were sometimes the centers of gang fights. Not a pleasant sight, but the slum area is never a pretty site. Last, but not least, he ended his beat at Max's gym. Max had been a prize fighter. He wasn't a really great fighter but certainly respectable. He saved a few dollars from his fights to buy the place. It wasn't much: a ring, a few punching bags, some wall mirrors, a pool table in the back room, a small training table, and a few vending machines were Max's sole investments. To Father Dillon it was more than just a place; it was a part of his life which had never really been fulfilled. At the end of his day's work, he would find himself a seat near the ring and watch the action. There were many times when he would just sit and stare at the vacant ring. Max was the type of guy who never questioned Father's actions. Max knew fight people. They had reasons to stare into space. Sometimes the stare could be interpreted to mean a lost fight or a lost ambition. If for no other reason, Father's presence added a little bit of class to the establishment. There weren't many great fighters who trained in the gym regularly, but there were a few who worked out now and then. This then was Father Dillon's daily routine. For a priest of sixty-seven it wasn't what one would call an easy job.

His parishioners wondered why he didn't ask the Bishop to give him a parish in a better section of the city, at least a place where he would have an assistant. What they didn't know was that Father Dillon wanted it this way. He didn't want the responsibility of having to hold large confirmation classes, write a church bulletin, post a building project, or put on a church bazaar in order to purchase a fancy new light fixture.

Six

In Father's Footsteps

THE DAYS PASSED and Dean became a regular around the priest's household. New paint replaced the old, flowers replaced weeds in the beds, and even the holy water basins seemed to shine.

"You've certainly brought new life into this place." Father Dillon was pleased. "Why, I wouldn't have believed a young lad could be so imaginative. Keep up this way, and there won't be any work left for you. You'll work yourself right out of a place. Just kidding, son, but I thought that you might at least ask for some break time. You might want to work out at the gym or swim at the Y. I have plenty of friends at these places, so it won't cost you a dime."

"Gee thanks, Father, but I keep pretty busy. When I'm not working around the house, I finger through some of the books in your library. I've found some interesting reading. I never realized there was so much to this religion bit. Rather interesting to read about what the scholars think of this Creator of ours. I was almost convinced that God didn't exist for guys like me. I guess I've been wrong all this while. So you see, I'm not wasting my time."

"Fine, Dean, but I thought that you might like to make the rounds with me some day. You might find it interesting, and maybe educational. It's like going to a state fair and seeing a lot of side shows. There are a lot of lost people in this world of ours. I've tried to help some of them, but I haven't always succeeded. Some people just don't want to see the light. They are nourished by the darkness. Oh, there I go again with my sermons. I'm sorry, son, but I get carried away once in awhile. If you ever want to come along, just say the word."

A few weeks passed. It was late in August, just before the local schools opened in September. The weather was humid, and the temperature hovered around the 100 degree mark. Few people frequented the streets, but the bars were gold nuggets to their owners. People even stayed away from church on days like this. Father Dillon finished the early morning Mass and seated himself for breakfast.

"Say, Father, remember that invite you gave me to make the rounds with you? Well, it's too hot to work, and I thought I might take you up on it.'"

"It's good to have you along, son." Mary winked at the priest, and he returned the gesture with a half smile. The two men left the house together.

"Where to first, Father?" Dean asked.

"I usually stop at the hospital. By the time I check with the receptionist to find out the number of Catholics, it's time for the other visitors to arrive. I visit the hospital daily. You never know when a person is in serious or critical condition."

"Do you just visit the Catholic patients?"

"Oh no, I try to comfort and greet all that I can get to see. I visit the various wards. The terminal cases are usually the worst. Some have been told by their doctors, and others, well, they just seem to know. A man of God, whether Catholic or Protestant, is always appreciated. There have been a few exceptions, but not many. I guess most of us realize the importance of our Almighty when we are on the last lap of life."

Dean would think about the priest's last remark. He would like to know more about the Almighty's importance. Dean opened the door to the hospital, and Father moved to the information desk. A nurse fingered through a number of cards. A hurried thank you, and the two moved toward the elevator.

"Four this time. Morning, Mrs. Zelinski." A middle aged woman turned her head from the pillow.

"Morning, Father. It's a boy this time. Fred will be so happy. After six girls, he's beginning to think the world has turned against him. We're going to name him Peter, after St. Peter, Father." The smile which spread across her face was reward enough for Father Dillon.

"You take care of yourself." Father Dillon blessed her and turned for the door.

"Thanks again, Father. I don't think Fred and me will be in to see you about all our troubles. This boy will fix everything."

"I never thought I would see a woman who looked so completely happy, Father. Why, she looked at you as if you had given her something priceless."

"True happiness is priceless, Dean. We're not long on this earth. Marriage can be hell for some, and then again it can be rewarding. Mrs. Zelinski knows that right now."

Dean gave the priest a quizzical look but made no reply. The sign read "no visitors" as Father Dillon pushed open the door to room 406.

"Do you want me to wait for you here?"

"No, no, come inside the door. It's all right." The elderly priest pressed the shoulder of a white haired man. The man turned ever so slowly in his bed to look at the priest and the boy. Dean would never forget the facial expression that came into view.

"How are you today, John? The nurses tell me that you're one of their best."

"Can't complain, Father Dillon. I hurt once in awhile, but I guess I'm to expect that. The doctor tells me that I might not make it this time." The man turned to Dean. "A friend of yours, Father?"

"Meet Dean Nelson, John. Dean stopped in on me one Wednesday night, and he's been with me ever since. I've got him doing some odd jobs for his keeping."

"Wednesday night! I remember the Wednesday I stopped in on ya. I wasn't sure if a priest or the devil met me at the door." The man managed a muffled laugh. "Still watch the fights?"

"You know better than to ask me that question. What else would I do on Wednesdays? You better get your rest now."

"Rest? It won't be too long and I'll be getting a lot of that. I'm not Catholic, Father, but I'd like to have—what do you Catholics call it—a confession, soon." With that the man turned his head toward the white wall.

Dean felt a lump in his throat. He reached the door, turned, and for just a minute he stared at the human form that faced the wall.

"He's a terminal cancer case. He's been in and out four times. Each time it takes a little more of his life. He never complains though." The priest noticed Dean's troubled look. He squeezed the boy's arm and said, "It's all right, son. He's an old man, and old men...." Father Dillon didn't finish his comment. "It seems as if he's already made his peace with someone. I'm a bit surprised that he wants me to talk with him."

Dean thought he understood about the old man's condition. What he also didn't understand was why the man had chosen Father Dillon and not someone else. Certainly there were others who frequented the hospital. When they left the hospital, Dean was still pondering this situation.

"Where to next, Father?"

"I thought that we might stop at the playground on seventy-second street. It isn't much of a playground, but it keeps the kids off the streets. I sure wish I could afford some new playground equipment though. The kids in those rich areas have new swings, teeter boards, and the works. You'd think the city lords would be more aware of the recreational apparatus available. It's in these neighborhoods where it does the most good."

Seven

Sluice – the Second Meeting

DEAN SWUNG OPEN the metal gate to the playground. A group of small children were kicking a ball across the rock covered ground. They hollered "hi" to Father Dillon when they saw him. In the far corner of the playground were some older boys. A puff of smoke made its hurried exit from the mouth of one of the younger boys.

"Well, if it isn't Dino. I see you're growing up fast?" A tall boy clad in Levis and an under shirt turned toward the priest. A cigarette protruded from his lips.

"Hi ya, Padre, who's that with ya, another of your touted altar boys? You really know how to pick em. I'll bet he hasn't smoked a fag in his entire life?"

"Meet Sluice Adams, Dean. He used to remember his manners, but of late he became one of the big boys. Next thing you know, he'll have the whole bunch in jail. I can recall when a young Adams boy came to church. That was before his father died. From what I hear now, that same boy strikes his mother. Must take a lot of courage to hit a woman, especially one that loves you."

"Shut up, Padre, or I'll shut ya up!" Dean whirled, directly blocking the path of the oncoming Sluice.

"Your little altar boy's gonna defend ya? Ain't that just great?" The three other boys moved in behind Sluice.

Before Dean could raise his hand, Father Dillon stepped squarely in front of Sluice. Their eyes met. The coldness and hate of the boy's eyes fell upon the sharp but understanding eyes of the priest. "Go ahead and hit away, boy. Get that hate out of your system." Sluice stared for a few moments.

"Come on. Hitting a padre wouldn't be fun any ways." The boys moved to another area of the playground.

"He really hates you, Father. Think he'll ever change?"

"Hate's a funny thing, son, but it isn't me he hates. It's what I stand for. He knows deep down in his heart that God and love have a strong foothold in this world. He'll find himself. He and the others are just mad at the world, not at God."

With those words Father Dillon closed the playground gate behind him. For a moment Dean was speechless. He had weighed every word that the priest had spoken. Had he been able to speak aloud, he might have said, "I want to believe that there is a God and love," but instead he simply uttered, "I guess you're right, Father Dillon."

"Thirsty? I usually stop at Sam's Bar for a bite to eat and a tap beer. Sam makes the best corn beef sandwich in the area. It's a little out of the way, but you'll get to meet some interesting people. I haven't stopped for a week or so, so Sam will be glad to see me."

"You know, Father Dillon, your work is quite interesting. You meet all types of people. When they're happy, your work is partially done, and when they have problems, whether they asked you or not, you're available for help. I bet you're never bored with your life."

"You know, I'd never looked at my life the way you just pictured it. Oh, I have my days. Take for example Sluice and his bunch. There isn't much that I can do for them until they want me to. Patience I've got. To be a priest, you have to have patience. Now that you mentioned it, I do live a different kind of life. Nope, I've never been bored. Tired, frustrated maybe, but never bored. Here's the place. It isn't too much of a place on the outside, but Sam's personality makes it warm within." The two entered the tavern.

Eight

Sam's Bar

"Well, if it isn't Matt Dillon, and who's the new sidekick, Chester?" The feminine voice caught Dean a little off guard. He wasn't expecting a woman, but there she sat at the bar. The close fitting blouse and skirt brought out the physical attributes of the woman. As she greeted them, she turned. A lace apron gave her a French-like appearance. Dean's eyes moved from the apron to the painted face. He had seen a few girls in his time. She wasn't unattractive, but it was her eyes that indicated the woman's secrets. Dean stood staring.

Father Dillon flashed a broad smile. "Well, Addie, if it isn't Addie Lawrence. I thought you were working the downtown area. You weren't here the last time I stopped in."

"Sam felt sorry for me. I needed the job and well, here I am. Who's your new sidekick?"

"Sorry! Dean Nelson, meet Miss Addie Lawrence."

"Hello."

"Hi, what can I get for the two of you?"

"What'll it be, Dean?"

"I'll have a glass of milk and two hamburgers, plain."

"Make mine the usual. Sam will know, and say, Addie, get me a glass of that tap beer." Addie penciled her pad and moved toward the kitchen.

"You seem to know the waitress, Father Dillon. Is she a member of your parish?"

"I wish she was, but no such luck. I remember Addie Lawrence when she came to town some eight years ago. She was looking for a respectable job. Jobs were hard to find then. No college background and just an average high school backing didn't qualify her for much. I can remember when she came to church on Sundays. She was one of the first at the communion rail, but with time, her visits became less frequent. I talked with her about it, but she, too, had been swallowed by the bigness of the city. The things she wanted, she couldn't afford. It happened the way it usually does. She got with the wrong crowd, and the first thing, she's pregnant. Oh, the guy would have married her, but he was a no good shifter. About the only thing that she did right was to come to me for advice. In this town, many unwed mothers have ways of getting rid of the life within. Addie, well she had a little more sense. She had her baby and put it up for adoption in a Catholic orphanage. Since that time, she kids me about being the

Matt Dillon of the westerns. I guess he helped people who needed help. I had hoped that Addie would return to the church, but instead, she became bitter with the world. She began frequenting the bars, working the streets, and losing whatever respectability she once had. This is the first time I've seen her for quite a while. Heard she was working the uptown district. She's still searching for her success. I only wish I could help her find it."

"Here's your food, padre, and your hamburgers."

"I suppose you're in another parish now, Addie."

"You never give up, do you, Father? I'm not going anymore. I just can't seem to find a reason for attending church. When you have done the things that I have done, and in such a short time, you give up hope of ever changing. I've hit the low rung on the ladder, I guess."

Addie was no longer the confident woman who greeted Father Dillon when they entered the tavern. She was sullen now. Her eyes lost the visible sparkle which Dean had first noticed. She moved her mouth as if to ask or say, "Anything else, Father?"

"No thanks. I'd like another tap, but some of the customers keep looking. I wouldn't want them to think that I had a problem. We've got to be moving along anyway. Mary will be waiting supper, and we still have a couple of stops to make before we head back home. Addie, if you ever want some conversation, the door of the...."

Addie interrupted before Father Dillon could

finish. "I know, Father, but when you reach the bottom of your rainbow, and you don't find your pot of gold…. Well, thanks anyway." With that she headed for the kitchen.

"That'll be $1.65," said Sam. "I couldn't help but hear what you were saying. I run a straight joint. I've got no call girls around, and Addie knows this. She's been pretty regular at her job. A woman adds a little class to the place. First time she gets out of line, and out she goes. She knows this. I think you're wasting your time about the church bit, though. She's a lost soul. She wants it that way."

"That's just it; we're all lost souls until we find ourselves. Sooner or later she's going to have to face reality. You have to work at life; it doesn't pop out and say here I am. My only hope is that she doesn't take the easy way out. It would be terrible to meet the new life dragging the old one behind."

FATHER DILLON DIDN'T say much as he shuffled slowly along the pavement. His bowed head indicated his frustration. "Yes, son, I've got a real interesting life. I win some of them, but most frequently I lose to my adversary. I wonder what he's got to offer."

Dean could see the strain in Father Dillon's face as he spoke. He knew then what he was looking for. It would take time, but after all he had youth. Realizing the tenseness of the present situation, Dean chortled, "Where to next? The city morgue?" The priest greeted his words with a quick glance. Dean's sense of humor had hit the wrong target.

"It's easy for you to joke about such things. You've had it hard, but you haven't been counted out. You're young and interested. When you lose that ambition, you'll know the battle of life."

Dean hadn't expected such a response. "I'm sorry, Father, I guess I spoke without thinking."

"It's not you, Dean; it's just that I feel so helpless when I come across people I can't help."

"What you don't seem to understand, Father, is that you do help all of these people. Just your presence and your conversation—what you stand for is sufficient. True, not all of your patients want your treatment, but they respect you, and that's what counts. They see in you what the good is really like. They don't have the strength to make the comeback, but you can't count them out either."

With that Dean gripped the shoulder of his companion. Father Dillon stopped and looked up at the boy. He smiled but didn't speak. The knot tying the two together was further fastened.

"Thanks, Dean, even a priest needs directing." With that Father Dillon pointed up the street. "Next stop is the downtown gym. There'll be a few friends that I want you to meet. Might be a few guys working out."

Nine

Max's Gym

A SIGN READ, "Work Out with Max." The two entered the gym. It wasn't much of a place. In one corner was a heavy punching bag; some weights cluttered the floor. A short piece of jumping rope lay coiled like a snake. A full length mirror reflected the full-sized ring that seemed to center the building. A few other pieces of apparatus littered the area. Dean glanced about the room. This wasn't the first time that he had visited a gym. The resin, the ropes, the center light—these were part of his past. Two fighters toyed with each other in the center ring. Dean noticed a short but muscular man sweeping the floor.

"Hey, Max, who are the pugs in the ring?" Father knew the raw fighter, the promising youth, and the over-the-hill pug. Max's place seldom housed the first two, and even the last didn't frequent the place very often.

Max Linder put aside his broom. He turned and the center light fell upon him. Two ugly scars were obvious above either eye. A fleshy nose and two cauliflower ears were the medals of the battles Max had fought. He had been no champion, but he had heart. He had never been knocked off his feet. The numerous scars about the face supported this boast. At fifty, Max still carried himself well. The gym gave him a chance to work a little. It kept him eating, and more importantly, sane. Most fighters lose their fortune before they enjoy any part of it. Well, Max lost his fortune early. A loan, a friend, and the gym kept Max off the canvas. He wasn't about to lose his last fight.

"Well, if it isn't Father Dillon. Haven't seen you around lately. I thought maybe you'd given up on the prize fighting game. Have you found that boy yet?" Max hadn't seen Dean enter with the priest.

"Still looking, Max, but I'll find him someday, and when I do, you'll train him." Max's broad grin showed the deep regard these two men had for each other. "Oh, Max, I've got someone I want you to meet. He stormed in on me one Wednesday night. Asked for a job, and he's been with me ever since. Dean, meet Max Linder, once a contender for the middle weight crown."

"Pleased to meet ya, Dean. Any friend of the Father's is a friend of mine. Ever wear the gloves? You're about the size of a welter weight. Good height, good reach..."

"My pleasure, Mr. Linder. I remember reading about you in some sport magazine. They even compared some of the newcomers to you. Yes, I boxed a little. Small town stuff, nothing more. Sure would like to work out in your gym sometime. That's if it's all right with Father Dillon."

Father Dillon had trouble containing his remarks. "Oh, I guess we can find time from your busy routine to get you to the gym a few times a week. Why, I might even join you. Haven't worked out in sometime. It might be good for me, too."

"We'd better be leaving, Dean. Mary gets upset when I'm not on time for supper. Thanks again, Max. Next time I'll stay longer. Might even be able to give some of your boys a few pointers. Remember, I used to fight." With that Father Dillon and Dean turned to leave.

"Bring the kid next time, Father. I'll see if he's got anything. Who knows, you might be walking with the next welter champ." Max flashed a quick smile.

"Thanks again, Mr. Linder. I'll sure take you up on that workout." Dean's eagerness came as somewhat of a shock to the priest. Oh, he wanted it to work this way, but he didn't expect such a move on their first outing.

"Well, Dean, what did you think of my route? I don't always make the same stops every time. Sometimes I visit the prison, the old folks' home, and the zoo, but like the old time milkman, I get to know many customers. I like it that way, and it seems the customers do, too."

"I really enjoyed myself, Father. I didn't realize that everyday life and people could be so interesting. I guess I've been a loner so long, I don't know what other people do anymore. I never really had time for people. When I had to work to eat, I would apply for jobs, but I never got too friendly with any of the employees. I used to sit off by myself and sip a coke or eat a candy bar. Most of the guys had home packed lunches. Someone to care for them. I guess they figured I was on the run or something. No sack lunches, no canned peaches, no homemade pie. I wasn't intended to be one of them. They knew it and so did I."

"Certainly someone must have invited you to his house for supper? Someone must have tried to make friends with you?"

"I wish I could say yes to your question. Never made any friends. Never went with a girl. So you see, Father, I'm what you call a perfect altar boy. There I go again feeling sorry for myself. I'm sorry, Father. "

"Forget it, son. You have a friend now. Unless I miss my guess, you'll make many more: Max, Mary, Dr. Browman, Sluice.... Eat supper, and you'll forget your problems. Mary's pie is heaven sent." Father Dillon chuckled quietly.

TEN

The New Altar Boy

A WEEK PASSED before Dean asked to make the rounds again. "I'd like to go with you again tomorrow. I thought I might buy some gym gear and take that workout that Max talked about. One other thing, I noticed that the altar boys have a habit of missing the early Mass. I thought maybe I could serve that Mass, that is, if you'd show me what I'm supposed to do."

"Serve Mass!" Father was elated. "Be my guest. It'll be a pleasure to show you. I was going to ask, but I guess waiting didn't do me too badly. We'll start in the morning. Very few attend, so we can run through a live Mass."

Bright and early the next morning, Dean stepped into a black vestment. He had searched the cabinet for one that would fit. He pulled on the garment, slipped his arms into the sleeves, and buttoned closed the opening. A white-laced, edged outer garment completed Dean's attire. He glanced into a nearby mirror. At first he felt a little uncomfortable, but it was only momentary. With hands behind his back, he passed back and forth in front of the mirror. He was very pleased with his appearance. More important was the feeling that he had inside. He felt close to something, someone.... His thoughts were interrupted as Father Dillon walked into the room.

"You may not know how to serve Mass, but you sure look like an altar boy."

Dean helped Father Dillon with his garments. He had found something that gave meaning to his life. He wouldn't run this time.

After preliminary instructions Dean was ready for his first performance. As he led the procession to the center of the altar, he recalled his boyhood days. The Sundays at Mass. Not being able to see above the crowd. Not knowing just what was going on. The sometimes suffocating heat. The longwinded sermons that sometimes sounded like his father and mother had done so many times. No, church didn't make much of an impression then, but it was different now. The soft carpet, the burning candles, the statutes, the closeness. Dean could feel the presence of something. Even the silence, something he had always dreaded, added the finishing touches to the atmosphere which pervaded the room. To think that he was now a part of it.

"Did you bring the cruets of wine and water?" whispered the priest. Dean was still gazing about him when with a little more force, Father Dillon asked the same question. "The water and wine. Did you forget...?"

Dean darted from the altar area, forgetting to genuflect. Within seconds, he was holding the water in one hand and the wine in the other. He remembered to bow his head upon completing this part of the Mass. He assumed his position at the foot of the altar. He began to wonder why Father had taken the little cloth while he had poured a little of the water over the priest's outstretched fingers. They didn't look dirty, but he reasoned that Father knew what he was doing. The Mass progressed. It was nearing the Communion part. Father had told him that he was to get a little plate from the table. He was to hold it under the chin of the persons at the altar rail. Again Dean's thoughts were interrupted by the priest. "The bell, Dean. Remember to ring the bell three times." He didn't see the signals, so he just rang it three rather lengthy times. Father turned rather abruptly, smiled, and continued. Dean was pleased. He cupped together his hands, genuflected, and went to the little table. The shining plate reflected his face. Only three people were at the rail. Dean held the plate under each of the chins. He watched every move. The little coin-like bread, the tongue extended, the prayer, and the expression on each of the receivers. They had something which Dean couldn't quite explain. He would try Communion someday, too.

"Well, Dean, you did a pretty good job out there today. A few more days and you'll be a top altar boy."

"Gee thanks, Father. I really enjoyed doing it. I've

got a few questions though. I don't understand all the things that you do. I'd like to know more about the Mass. It sort of shook me up when you started washing your hands like that. Did you get something sticky on them?"

"Just a few crumbs. I'll explain it some other time."

Eleven

Two Life Changing Events

"**Going to join** me for my rounds?" the old priest asked. "I thought I might visit the same places we visited a week ago. That's if it is all right with you?"

"Just fine. I enjoyed the first tour. It'll give me a chance to get a little better acquainted. After all, if I'm going to stay a little while, I should make a few friends." Dean felt good when he said "Friends."

Mrs. Zelinski wasn't there anymore. She had gone home to her husband and children. Father Dillon opened the door to room 406. The man did not turn as he had done at their first meeting. He was worse this time. A nurse entered the room and whispered something to the priest, then left again.

"It's me, John, Father Dillon. I've come to visit with you again." John was dying. He knew, Father Dillon knew it, and Dean sensed it. The searching eyes, the fear, the ever increasing pain. John was climaxing his struggle for life. One could tell that he was ready to give up. Dean realized that it was the pain that makes one forget about life.

"It's funny, but God must have known I wanted a priest," murmured the old man. "I knew He wouldn't let me down. I knew that if I endured the pain just a little while longer, it would be easier. Already the pain is easing off." Father Dillon took the outstretched hand. "Remember, Father, I said I had something to tell you, my confession. I don't think I can wait any longer." There wasn't time for Dean to leave the room. "Give me strength to face death. My life had the good and the bad. I guess I had my share of lies, and I was selfish with greed. I know of late that I've changed my course of life. I could be lying again just to win favor, but a person just doesn't lie in this battle. Forgive me, Father, I'm sorry for what I've done. I love you, God...." Dean saw Father Dillon make the sign of the cross. The old man's hand gripped, groped, and then went limp.

"Our Father who art in Heaven, hallowed be Thy name ...." The prayer from Father's lips filled the room. Dean lowered his head. The priest took a little vial from his bag, opened it, dabbed his finger, and proceeded to make little crosses on the forehead and other places on the old man. Dean had a strange feeling in the pit of his throat. His eyes moistened. He had been a witness to death, the end of life, or the beginning. Dean and Father left the room. They made a few other visits and then started down the stairs from the hospital.

"He's won his battle, son. He won't have to suffer anymore. I'm sure of that."

Dean didn't hear the priest's last words. He was thinking of his own life. He, too, had been selfish. He cared only about himself. It wasn't too late to change. He was young, and what's more he wasn't dying with cancer. The old man had been his signal. He would change. How he would change!

"How about the playground? Want to try your luck at it again? With luck we might just run into Sluice and his group again."

A few children ran up to the priest.

"Hi, Father, how about playing with us? Leo's always making up rules as he goes along. With you playing, we might have a chance."

"Okay with me. You don't mind, Dean? I'll just play a little while. You might wander around the grounds. Make a few friends. Stay away from Sluice and that bunch though."

Dean kicked the little stone in front of his shoe. With hands in his pockets, he walked aimlessly to the far end of the playground. He was still thinking of the old man. He didn't see the long haired youth's leg. Dean went sprawling to the ground.

"Would you look at the little altar boy? What ya doing playing marbles on the ground. Where's your bodyguard? Better still, where's your halo?" Dean had pushed himself into a crouched position. He glared at Sluice. "What's the matter, little man, you scared or something? Let 'im up."

The others distanced themselves from where Dean was sitting. By this time Father Dillon had witnessed the gathering. He pushed himself to where Sluice stood. "Well, well, well, if it isn't the protector of man's soul, the servant of God." Dean leaped from his half crouch like a cat on its prey. He struck away at that sneering face. His blows carried with them a little of Dean's hatred for Sluice and his gang. Sluice was the hate of the world. Dean wasn't about to let anyone talk to his priest friend the way Sluice had talked.

"Damn it! Don't just stand there. Pull the monster off me. He'll kill me!" yelled Sluice. Two of the boys jumped into the battle. Dean swung from all angles. Some of his blows hit flesh that smashed like melons being dropped. "Call him off, Father. We've had enough of him." Father Dillon grabbed Dean from behind. His vice-like grip held Dean at bay.

"I'll kill 'em! Let me go. No one talks to you that way."

"Easy, boy, he's not worth fighting over. Come on, cool down." The priest's voice eased the situation.

Dean relented just a little. His breathing returned to normal.

"He's a killer, not an altar boy. Can't take a little joke." With that, Sluice and his followers left the scene.

Dean wanted to let loose with just one more punch. He'd close that wise guy's big mouth for a long time.

"Can't say you look like the same lad that served me at Mass this morning," uttered the priest.

"I'm sorry, Father Dillon. It's just that I've seen that type before. Talking is a waste of time. The only thing they know is the fist. I've had my turn with others."

"Say, you really know how to use those fists. That right of yours is lightning fast. You throw straight punches. Yes, you really got the hands." The priest gripped the arm of his youthful companion. A bond, stronger than friendship, was in that grip.

Twelve

Father's Boxing Career

The two walked slowly away from the recreational area. After they walked a few blocks, the friendly sign, "Work Out with Max" flashed before them.

"If you don't care to workout, Dean, I'll understand."

Dean fired back a quick reply, "Ok, Father, why wouldn't I want to workout?"

"Just kidding, boy, but I thought I'd make the comment just the same." Father Dillon's eyes sparkled with his comment. He shouldered his way past two would be spectators, and then held open the door for Dean. As they entered Max's gym, Dean tapped Father's shoulder.

"Your interest in Wednesday night fights and your interest in Max seem somewhat related. How come you like boxing so well? I also noticed some of the scars on your face. You were either in a car wreck or you were in sports."

Father Dillon looked squarely into Dean's face. "I was a promising boxer when I was your age. I had had some fifty amateur bouts. I had won the welter weight Golden Glove Tournament; shortly after that, I turned pro. I had a record of 30 wins, 2 losses, and 18 knockouts. I was known in the ring as Jimmy (Hawk) Dillon. I never lost as an amateur, so I was expected to win in the professional ranks. My manager and trainer, Bruce Lehan, had never fought for a title, but he had had many fights with the top fighters in his weight division. Like most fighters, Bruce never got a shot at the title. At any rate, Bruce taught me everything he knew about boxing, about boxing politics, and the life of a promising fighter. Without Bruce, my career would have ended early.

"After about twenty professional fights, I moved up in the rankings to the sixth best of the middle weights. Two more fights and I would probably get a shot at the champ. At any rate, Bruce got me a bout with Jim Robinson. Robinson was ranked just below me, but he was a tough, brawling-type fighter, and Bruce felt that I should meet someone like that, since the champ was a similar fighter. The match was made for a ten round fight. I was in the best shape of my life the night I stepped into the ring against Robinson. For eight rounds, I jabbed and hit, and I was ahead on points going into the ninth round. Though I had been warned by Bruce, I got caught in the corner. I tried to clinch, and when I did that, our heads hit accidentally. In seconds, I felt the trickle of blood run down my forehead and into my eye. I got through the round. As I sat in my corner, Bruce and my cut man did the best they could to close the gaping wound. I was fortunate that the ring doctor didn't check the cut, or the fight would have been stopped. I got through the ninth, but punches from Robinson opened up the cut over my eye even bigger. The ring doctor was called by the referee to examine my eye. It didn't take a skilled doctor to know that I could not continue the fight, and since the cut was accidental, Robinson was awarded the win.

"It took over two months for the cut to heal. I still worked out daily, but I didn't do any sparring. After the cut healed, Bruce asked if I would like to fight Robinson again. Since I was ahead of Robinson in our previous fight, I jumped at the chance to fight him again. The sport pages in the daily newspaper talked about my continued plans to fight a warm up bout before meeting the champ. The fight was made. I touched Robinson's gloves as the fight began. Again it was a ten rounder, and I was ahead after eight rounds, but unlike the previous fight, Robinson caught me with a smashing punch to the previously cut eyebrow. It was almost like someone had sliced me with a straight razor. The blood trickled and then ran out of the gaping wound. Needless to say, I was a beaten fighter when I sat in my corner and heard the ring doctor say, 'He can't continue the fight.'

"That was the end of my fighting career. Another

loss, but this time, it was also the end of my hopes, my dream. I never laced on the gloves again. Now, son, you know why I watch the Wednesday night fights and why I visit Max's gym. My dream is still out there, and Dean, you could very well be the person to help me fulfill that dream." With that the priest walked briskly ahead, greeted Max, and the two shook hands.

Thirteen

A Serious Workout

Dean now realized another part of the puzzle was slowly being pieced together. He knew that the priest had very special plans for him. Dean wasn't quite ready to fill the huge gap in Father Dillon's life, but he also knew that he couldn't let the old priest down. He would visit Max's gym daily; he would up his daily run to six or eight miles. He would begin preparing for at least one of the two highlights that his promising future held.

"Hi, Padre, long time no see," bellowed Max. "What'll it be? How about a beer? See ya still got the lad with ya." Max walked over to a small refrigerator and got the priest his beer.

Father Dillon plunked himself down on one of the stools near the ring. "Yes, sir, a cold beer sounds real good. How about you, Dean?"

"Nothing, thanks. Say, Max, I've brought some gear. Mind if I work out?"

"No, siree. You'll find a towel and a locker in the far corner by the drinking fountain."

Dean left the two and headed in the direction of the locker area.

"That's some boy, Father."

Father Dillon made no reply. After a moment he said, "You ought to see him with his fists! Boy's really fast and straight."

Max looked a little bewildered at the priest's response, but he continued picking up the conversation.

"Oh, he's a fighter, huh? You're still lookin' for that one special boy?"

Again there was no reply.

The boy reappeared, but this time he wore some faded purple trunks and a rather grey-looking sweatshirt. "Mind if I work the big bag?" Dean shouted.

"Go right ahead. When ya get tired of the bag, climb into the ring. I've got a boy about your weight that's itching to get a little workout. He won't hurt ya; he just wants to work up a sweat before he showers." Max continued, "What weight do you normally fight at?"

"I'm somewhere in the 140's, give or take a few pounds. Most of my amateur fights were in the welter weight division. I fought a few times at heavier weights, but that's when I wasn't in shape. Doing the odd jobs for Father and eating Mary's great food certainly may have added to my weight. If I ever decided to fight again, I would certainly fight as a welter weight."

Max gasped. He knew that Father had had some fights at that weight. It would indeed be a coincidence if Dean ever decided to lace up the gloves again. With that Max climbed into the ring.

Dean looked in the direction of the center ring. A curly headed youngster about his size and age moved about the ring. Dean could tell that the boy had been in the ring before. The boy moved easily to his left and then to his right, feinting, darting, and throwing punches at an imaginary target. The boy looked really sharp, thought Dean, as he spread the ring ropes apart so he could climb into the ring. By this time Max had moved closer to the center of the ring.

"Jim, I want you to meet Dean. Dean's been helpin' Father." Jim nodded a friendly, "Hello."

"How about going a few rounds with him?" continued Max. "Go easy, though, I don't want the boy getting hurt."

"Ya know me, Max, I just like to workout." Then Jim retreated to a neutral corner. Both boys had been given 20 ounce gloves. Father Dillon finished putting the gloves on his boy. Max sounded a bell, and both boys went to the center of the ring. Father was surprised to see Dean extend his gloves so that they touched the outstretched gloves of Jim. Dean had been in the ring before. He wasn't simply a newcomer. He knew the inner area of the ring; he knew the smell of resin, and he knew the scent of battle. Father wondered if Jim had the same thoughts.

Both boys were superbly built. Jim, the taller of the two, made the first move. He crashed two quick jabs into Dean's face. Dean winced, blinked his eyelids, and then flashed a disturbed smile. The jabs seemed to trigger Dean's moves. With a whip-like movement, his gloved hands engulfed Jim's head. Jim was moving away, so the two blows had no telling impact, but they did alert Jim to the opponent before him. Jim wasn't the only boxer in the ring. His opponent was fast and most certainly experienced. Jim knew he had his work cut out for him. He respected this "new boy." Jim worked in close and threw two punches to Dean's midsection. He was hoping that this would bring Dean's head down so he could follow with his uppercut. Dean knew what Jim was attempting. He dropped his head a little, but as he did, he let go with a straight right. The right caught Jim right on the chin. Had the gloves been regulation, Jim would have been down for a count.

"That is quite a right hand you've got, Dean."

"Those slaps you smacked into my face weren't exactly love taps," quipped Dean.

Arms around each other's necks, the two boys laughed and headed for the showers.

"You hit the jackpot this time, Padre. He's cool. Moves like a cat. Good hands, and boy, that right was clean and straight. He could really be something!" beamed Max. "Wouldn't mind training him."

"You really think he's got something? You're not

just feeding my ambition?" Father Dillon gave Max a hurried but meaningful look.

"Ya know me, Father. I wouldn't lie to a priest, maybe to a guy, but never a priest. In that brief time in the ring, I noticed that both of his hands were held low. If he's going to be a prize fighter, we'll have to work on that upper body protection. He's got to learn to keep his chin tucked more into his shoulder and his gloves up to protect him from right hand punches. He also threw punches with his feet almost parallel. He's got to bring the right foot back a little so when he throws his right, it'll have force in it. On the positive side were his straight jabs with either hand. He jabbed three times with that left and followed with that right hand, and man, that's not seen too much in young fighters."

That was enough for Father Dillon. Another piece of his puzzle had fallen into place.

DEAN FREQUENTED MAX'S gym in the following weeks. When his work was finished at the priest's house, Dean would find his way to the gym. His route to the gym included a visit to the playground, a hurried hello to people on the street, a stop at the local jail, a frequent visit to the hospital, and then on to the gym. Dean's visits became almost as significant as Father Dillon's. Like Father, Dean didn't visit because of obligation. He wanted to help those who couldn't help themselves. Life had a new meaning, and God played such an important part. Dean knelt at his bed. He touched his fingers first to his head, then to his chest, to his left and finally to his right. As he stared off into the darkened room, Dean thought of his chance meeting with Father Dillon. His vision flashed back to the smile on Mrs. Zelinski's face. He recalled the troubled face of the dying old man. He wouldn't forget those events. Sluice's face was also in his memory. Dean knew that Sluice was also his challenge.

"Dear God, help me to understand Thy ways. I don't want to hurt Father Dillon, but I cannot contain my feelings. Please give me strength and direction. Amen." Dean crossed himself, pulled back the covers, and climbed slowly into bed.

Not too distant from Dean's room, Father Dillon put away his pipe. He likewise prepared for bed. Slipping to his knees, he started to pray. His whispered words were hardly audible. "I have served Thee to the best of my limited ability. I have never asked for personal gains. My material wants are few. You know that my one dream, selfish as it may seem, was to be a prize fighter champion. Not that I haven't enjoyed my priestly life, but...." With that, Father Dillon cupped his hands, bowed his head, and finished his prayers in silence.

The next morning, both men awoke earlier than usual. "Funny thing, but I just couldn't sleep last night," said Dean, as he munched a strip of bacon. "Tried remembering all that I was thinkin about, but it was all sort of mixed up. Guess I'm getting too involved with things around me."

"You weren't the only one, son," replied the priest. "I kept rolling from one side to the other. I could understand if I had had one of Max's corn beef sandwiches before retiring. Can't blame it on that. Just the same, something must have been bothering me. I'm hardly what you'd call a light sleeper."

Dean searched Father's face, but the answer which he had hoped for did not come forth from the priest. "Well, Dean, should we get ready for Mass?"

Dean pushed in his chair, flashed a brief smile, as if to say, "That's okay for now, but we're going to have to sit down soon."

Dean got into his altar boy garments, and watched carefully as Father put on each of his vestments. Dean was always close by to help the old priest get ready to say the morning Mass. Father walked up the two steps to the altar; Dean kneeled on the first step and watched closely each and every movement the priest made. He wanted to understand better just what was taking place. He no longer needed the priest to tell him to ring the bell. He knew his cues and rang the bell three times. He brought the priest the water and wine. He would watch very closely the priest's every move. Father slowly poured a bit of the water and some of the wine into his shining chalice, said something in Latin, and turned back to the altar. Dean watched him carefully as he broke the wafer, placed the pieces into his mouth, and sipped gently the wine. Dean noticed that the priest's eyes were closed gently during this ceremony. He looked at the priest's closed fingers, and for just a few moments Dean felt a strange sensation; it was almost as if Dean, for a moment or two, had entered a strange but different world. He wasn't at all suspicious, but he thought that he was in a different world, a heavenly space. He wished to share these sensations with Father Dillon. What would the priest think? What would he say?

The Mass ended, and the two walked slowly into the sacristy. Father Dillon took off his vestments. Dean, close by, helped with the disrobing. He felt the softness of the garments. For just a few seconds, Dean seemed to press them to his heart. The priest was too busy to notice this small but significant move.

Fourteen

A New Manager

"**You going to** the gym today? Thought I might join you. Max tells me that you've been working out just about every day. You certainly must like Max's company, or better still, you must like the smell of the gym."

"Father, I've been fixing to ask you something that's been bothering me for a long time. I don't know how to say it, but, well, you've been so darn fair with me and all. Here I'm eating food from your table, visiting your friends, working out in the gym...."

"That's quite all right, son. I told you when you first came here that you could stay as long as you wanted to. In fact, son, I'm proud that you decided to stay as long as you have. Makes me think that you like it here. We don't have all of the comforts of home, but we share what we have."

"It isn't that, Father, but I keep thinking about my future. I can't go on living off you. Sooner or later I've got to strike out on my own. I've thought about getting another job or moving on. Somehow I just can't get myself to leave. This is why I must sit down and talk about my future, what I want to be, I mean."

"I could tell you were a little disturbed by the way you've been acting lately. I've seen the change which has come over you. You don't seem to be as interested in Mass and the hospital visits. It's the itch to get back in the ring again, isn't it? Don't apologize, boy, I could tell it the first time you climbed into the ring with Jim. You want to be a boxer. You want my permission to give up your duties with me. I know just how you feel. I remember when I was your age. Had the same ideas. I often thought I might make it big in the ring. Never did, but that doesn't change a person's desire." Father Dillon was smiling as he made his last statement.

Dean had a rather disappointed look on his face. The priest hadn't understood him at all. He couldn't bear to hurt the older man. He would have to tell him soon, but he knew if he did now, the old priest would have a second dream shattered. Somehow he had to make the priest understand. He had to tell him what he really wanted, but it could wait. How long Dean didn't know. The boy's thoughts were interrupted by the priest's leading question.

"How about the two of us teaming together? You absorb the punishment in the ring, and I'll absorb the punishment outside. We'll make a good team. Together we can realize an old man's dream. What I'm saying, kid, is I'd like to manage you. The colors of a priest in the corner of a prize fighter won't hurt the box office none either. I'm sure the bishop will grant me permission."

Father Dillon was bubbling over with enthusiasm. Dean hadn't observed the priest in such a state ever before. He knew that Father Dillon was getting a second chance at his youthful ambition. He couldn't, he wouldn't let the priest down. He knew that God wouldn't let him down either.

"Gee, Father, that's just great. I thought maybe you'd be disappointed with me. Thought you might think I was putting myself above my duties to you and the others."

"Some of us get the call to do God's work, son. Still others serve in other capacities. So it is with you, Dean. Someday you may be the champion of the world. People will look up to you. Children will want your autograph. So you see, you'll be doing God's work also."

Dean smiled and seemed to give approval to the priest's words. Dean's mind was filled with many things far removed from Max's gym. He began to recall some of the experiences he had had as a boy. He remembered going to church; he remembered going to Mass, but he also remembered that he didn't understand what went on during those brief visits. He didn't remember his parents telling him about being baptized, but he must have been because he did remember the white shirt, the tie, the black pants, and the first Communion and the camera photos, but that was all he could remotely remember about his religious activities. Had he ever had a confession? Would that be important? Should he ask the priest about the meaning of Communion? It seemed all new to him. He would watch Father's every move the next time he served the Mass.

WEEKS PASSED. MAX'S gym became his second home. The word had gotten around that Father Dillon, in addition to his priestly duties, had become the manager of a promising young boxer. Max had never had it so good. His place was like an auction hall. Reporters, ex-pugs, free loaders, business men, and men of the cloth milled about. Max had to hire extra help. The headlines of the Dispatch read: "Local priest manages prize fighter." The Tribune flashed, "Father Dillon's altar boy turns to prize fighting." The sight of a priest and a young, promising fighter gave new life to a blighted sports page. Father Dillon scheduled regular workouts. He answered the queries of the many reporters. He wrapped his arm around Dean's neck when the flashbulbs popped. Jimmy (Hawk) Dillon, the young promising boxer, was reliving what he had always wanted in his youth. In between reporters' questions and supporting pats on his back, Dean observed all. Though he was depicted as a "promising young boxer" Dean had matured considerably. He was no longer young. In years, yes, but not in thoughts. In a way, he, too, was serving a worthwhile purpose. His life was giving meaning to another. He tilted his head slightly. Someone close by might have heard him say, "Thank you for guiding me; thank you, dear God."

Dean, Max, the trainer, and the managing priest had become celebrities almost overnight. When Dean and Father Dillon made their visits to the hospital, the Y, the playground, and the jail, they were hailed with. "When's your first fight? Will it be televised?"

"Killer or angel?" screamed an inmate of the local jail. Father Dillon would simply shrug his shoulders, "Just wait until you see him."

Father Dillon had received permission from the bishop to pursue his new course in life, a life that took on new significance. His sermons were more potent and more pointed. Parishioners who hadn't attended church except at Christmas flocked to the little church. There were even communicants at the early morning Mass. Father liked to believe that they were there to serve God, and not simply to observe his altar boy boxer. Whatever their reasons, the priest responded reverently. His priestly life took on new meaning. He was finally ready to accept his service to God. He saw through the publicity, the flashy headlines, and the friendly clasps of his hands. This life was simply too easy, too artificial. He liked it, but he liked his other life better. Yes, he would have to have his talk with Dean.

"WHAT DO YOU think, Max; is he ready?"

"Well, Padre, I've been working with the kid for the past few weeks. Remember what I said about the way he held his arms low and wasn't tucking in his chin the way he should? Well, we've corrected those problems. We've also worked on his stance when he throws that special right. He's been a quick learner. He knows that when he jabs that he has to jab and move. I especially warned him that after he jabs or throws his right that he should never go straight back, or he could get hit on the button with a straight right or left. I told him about using a right cross, and we went carefully over his foot movements. I told him to always keep his heels up when moving. He's a great listener, and he's a quick learner. You should see him work on the speed bag, the heavy bag, the skipping and jumping ropes, the toe touches, the sit ups, the pushups, the medicine ball, and the weights. I have a special program each time that he comes into the gym. We even discussed how to clinch his opponent if and when he needs to do that. I've warned him about fighting off the ropes or getting caught in the ring's corners. We've spent hours watching films. He's been in the ring several times with some of the other promising fighters, and we've worked daily on improving his style, his moves, his punches, and even his clinches. He's something quite special. Your dreams may be realized with this kid. He and Jim have become close friends. I might also add that having him in the gym has had an impact on some of the other street kids. Remember that kid, Sluice, and his buddies? Well, they've been visiting the gym weekly. In fact, the leader, Sluice, might be another fighter prospect, if he could just control his temper. Right now, he's a rough-cut diamond, but with the proper training and some personal dedication, he could make it. Thanks to you, Father, and especially to Dean, my gym has become a new and meaningful place. Won't be too long, and I'll have to fix up the place."

Fifteen

The First Fight

"**Dean Nelson fights** Bob Tison. Tison is undefeated in his last five fights. A win for Tison will put him with the ranked fighters," read the Tribune.

"How do you feel, Dean? Nervous? Can't say I blame you. You know everyone in the parish plans to be at the arena. Why, that's all I hear on the streets these days. Remember that Sluice and his bunch? They're all working out at Max's place. They want to be fighters, and that at least keeps them off the streets. Saw Addie the other day. She's purchased a ticket for the fight. I heard that she met a real nice guy who wants to marry her. Would you believe it, he's Catholic? Looks like she'll be coming to Mass again."

"Father, remember that talk I wanted to have with you? Well, it can wait until after the next few fights. I know that you have enough on your mind with the reporters, with Max and the others. Why don't we plan to have that talk when things settle down? Why, at this point we don't know just what's going to happen. Could be my opponent will get lucky, and my professional boxing career could come to an abrupt end. Oh, I'm not being negative, but it's been a long time since I have been in the ring. Ten rounds with even an average to poor fighter could be an eternity for me."

The priest looked at him, but Dean knew that the priest didn't pay much attention to what he was saying. Father Dillon was too much engrossed in the coming fight that would partially fill his dream.

"IN THIS CORNER, wearing the purple trunks and hailing from Minneapolis, Minnesota, weighing in at 147 pounds, the promising newcomer, Dean Nelson," bellowed the ring announcer. "In the blue corner, also at 147 pounds, from Detroit, Michigan, undefeated, with a record of 5 wins, no losses, and 3 knockouts, Bob Tison."

The two fighters, along with their trainers, walked slowly to the center of the ring. Rich Reynolds, the referee, briefly discussed the rules. "No low blows. Watch head butting. Break clean when I say break. Touch gloves, and let's have a clean fight." They touched gloves and moved back to their respective corners."

Max, in a soft-spoken voice, uttered, "You have the skills and the attitude to win this one. Remember, everything you do comes off your jabs. Keep the left hand or right hand jabbing constantly. Jab straight and jab often."

"Father Dillon echoed much the same advice, adding, "Keep moving, stay off the ropes, and don't allow Bob to get you in the corners. Good luck, Dean!"

The bell rang for round one. The two fighters met in the center of the ring and touched gloves. Father Dillon had waited many, many years for this part of his dream to happen. He knew this would be his last chance to be a part of what he so missed in his youthful days. Both fighters circled at center ring. Dean, the taller of the two, had heard the ref's instructions, but his eyes wandered around the ring. Sluice and his gang sat directly behind his corner. Sluice flashed a victory sign to Dean. Scanning ringside hurriedly, Dean's eyes fell upon Addie and the middle aged gent next to her. They held hands. Addie's eyes were no longer dull. They sparkled like a debutant about to be introduced to society. Addie saw Dean's quick glance. A slight nod and a smile assured Dean that Addie had found a new course in life. To think he had had a small part in redirecting what Father Dillon called the lost soul. "They hate the world, not God." Dean recalled those words. His thoughts were interrupted by Bob's lightning fast jabs to his face. He wasted no time in moving to the side and back from Bob, but Bob moved faster. Dean felt the jabs time and again. He tucked in his chin and brought up his gloves to shelter his face and upper body. He tucked in his elbows, further protecting his ribs and mid-section. Dean focused on Bob and flicked out three jabs of his own. The bell rang and Dean found himself sitting on the stool in his corner.

"What were you glaring at in the early part of the round?" Max asked. "Leave your thoughts for another day." Max knew Tison. He had seen Bob fight his last outing. Max leaned over to Dean. "Watch that right hand; he'll get you thinking he's a southpaw and then bang, he brings up the right hand."

Dean was hearing Max's words but not listening to what Max was saying. He was still thinking of Addie, Sluice, the hospital, the jail, the gym, and the playground as the bell sounded for round two. Tison had heard of this altar boy boxer. He knew Father Dillon, and he knew Max wouldn't be training a loser. Tison flicked two left jabs into Dean's face. A third jab caught the tip of the altar boy's nose. Dean was still not concentrating as a fighter should do. He was still thinking about Mass, Communion, confession, and all of the things which had brought him understandable happiness. His thoughts were interrupted by Bob's crushing right hand. Like a feathered arrow, it struck its target. Dean's knees buckled and his right knee creased the canvas. "One, two, three, four." A hand flashed with each count. For a few fleeting moments, Dean felt like he was joining his hospital friend John in the Heavenly unknown. He shook his head; his eyes cleared. He saw Max and Father Dillon barking for him to get up. The count reached nine, and like a pheasant flushed from its hiding place, Dean lurched to gain man's upright posture. Tison was not about to be denied a quick knockout. Dean felt the jab again and again, and he knew the right would follow. No longer was he the altar boy, the thinker. Old man John had won his battle in death, but Dean's life and hope were ahead of him. He was not about to lose again; he couldn't let Max, Father Dillon, and the others down. He had known defeat early in his young life. Feeling sorry for himself wasn't the answer. He tucked his chin in closer to his left shoulder. This was his chance for a new and meaningful life. Tison let loose with another right hand, but this time Dean expected the move. With the right hand up, he caught Bob's blow and scored with his own left hand as the bell ended round two.

"You had us both worried, son," barked Max. "Why, you looked as if you were in another world when Tison's right hit you," Max blurted. "You gotta move and hit and move some more. You're not Gene Fullmer out there. Dean understood this time. Father touched Dean's sore nose with a cotton bud. The bell sounded for round three. Dean hurriedly remembered a Gene Fullmer who had been an outstanding fighter and champion, and he understood what Max was saying. "You're not a knockout fighter; you must hit and move."

The bell sounded, and Tison roared across the ring. He didn't want his taller opponent to warm to the situation. His left jabs battered Dean. "If only Tison would let up for just a little while, I might be able to get into the rhythm of the fight," thought Dean. He managed to clinch Bob, and for just a few seconds, Dean was able to collect his thoughts. The referee separated the fighters, but this time Dean's head had cleared; he was back in the ring; he was fighting for his very life. He remembered how hard and fast he had hit Sluice when Sluice had bad-mouthed Father Dillon. Dean moved in on Tison. He remembered Max had said, "Everything comes off the jabs." Dean jabbed once, twice, and a third time, but he didn't throw the right. Tison had a quizzical look on his face. He knew this was not going to be a one-sided fight. The bell ended the round.

The fourth and fifth rounds went much the same way, but Dean could see that his punches were slowing down his more experienced opponent. He would change his strategy in round six. He would try to move in closer so he could get some body shots. He remembered that in some of his amateur fights going to the body had its impact. It might just bring down Tison's hands long enough to get in a telling right hand.

Tison came out much slower in the sixth. Dean had

more of a chance to gather his thoughts. He managed to get in close and pounded both the right and left hands into Tison's stomach. He knew the punches hurt Tison. Tison was moving away. He would throw a jab or two, but these lacked the zip or force they had in the first four rounds. Dean went back to his jabs, and sure enough, Tison, thinking that Dean was going to the body, brought his gloves down just enough to protect his mid-section. Tison never saw the right hand hit him. He reeled backward, and Dean moved in. Tison, depending on all of his boxing skills, managed to tie up Dean. When the referee parted the two, Dean saw the cut, the flow of blood from the cut above Tison's left eye. Father Dillon also saw the cut. He had a flashback to his fighting days and his two brutal cuts, but it wasn't Dean who was bleeding. He silently and quickly thanked God. Dean disliked cutting up an opponent, but the cut was legitimate. It hadn't been caused by a head butt. The referee went briefly to Tison's corner to check the severity of Tison's cut. Tison's cut-man worked furiously to stop the flow of blood.

Round seven sounded. There was no rush by Tison this time. Though he was a fighter with a knockout punch, he was also a wise fighter. He knew that he would have to box if he hoped to get through the next three rounds. Dean had had the killer instinct earlier in his amateur fights, but this instinct was based on his dislike for life, for survival. Father Dillon, Mary, Sam, Max, Addie, Sluice, John, Jeb and Dr. Browman, and all the others had given him a new look at life.

He no longer had the killer's instinct. He would jab and jab, but he made no attempt to reopen the huge cut above Tison's left eye. Tison realized what was happening. He realized that this altar boy fighter was humane. The bell sounded, and Tison went back to his corner, blood still flowing from the open cut. The referee again went over to Tison's corner, but this time he signaled the ring doctor to check Tison's eye. It didn't take but a few glances and the ring doctor declared the fight was over. Dean had won on a TKO. The ref motioned the two fighters to the center of the ring, and he raised Dean's hand in victory. The spectators were quick to show their appreciation of Dean's efforts in his first fight. The crowd was roaring.

Father and Max kept pounding Dean's back. "You did it, kid; one right hand and you won the fight." Father Dillon put his arm around Dean's neck. The two had found the keys to their future lives. It was the right time for Dean to say, "We need to have a serious talk before or after the next two fights."

"Sure, sure, Dean, anything you say. I was sort of hoping you'd want to make a confession before you embarked on your new life. It'll make you feel better inside. Don't worry. I understand."

Sixteen

Jose Zapata

DEAN CONTINUED TO be an altar boy, but after each early morning Mass, and even before they had their breakfasts, Father and Dean would go into his office and Dean would ask questions about the Mass, the Communion, the confession and about death. Father seemed to know just what to say to his young admirer. He explained why he closed his eyes during the breaking of the wafer, the breaking and eating of the Body of Christ, and the drinking of the Wine, the Blood of Christ. Dean asked about the anointing of the dying. Again, the priest explained fully the anointing and its meaning. Dean asked about the Baptism ceremony, and Father told him about Original Sin and that a Baptism was one of the steps which brought a child or an adult who was baptized into God's world. Dean was most concerned about the confessional and the confession. Father told him that the confessional was a very special, private place where the priest could listen carefully and thoughtfully to persons who had sinned in the eyes of God. Father mentioned the absolution near the end of the confession and the purpose behind penance. Father impressed upon him that a true confession was one where the sinner truly was sorry for his or her sins. The penance and the absolution were part of the confessional process. In reality, the sinner was in the presence of his God when citing his sins. The priest was simply acting as God's servant on earth. So carefully did Father Dillon explain each of his responses, Dean had even fewer questions for their next conversation.

Dean was anxious to learn who his next fight would be with. He never let up, even after winning his fight with Tison.

"We have to go back to the basics again," said Max. "You can't ever forget the fundamental things in boxing: your stance, the position of your arms and elbows, your rhythm. You've got to block out the distractions which you seemed to have in your last fight. If you lose focus, if you forget our fight plan, you'll join the ranks of the defeated, and your promising career could come to a screeching halt. I know; I've been there; Dillon also knows; he, too, has been there. You're young; you're strong, fast, and ambitious, and you're technically smart, but you will need all of those attributes if you ever hope to be a champion. One glaring mistake, and your career hopes come to an abrupt end."

For some reason or other, Dean felt that Max knew his very private secret, but how was that possible?

Could Max have watched him so closely in the last fight that Max knew when he looked out and saw all of his friends and his admirers that he was thinking about this and not thinking about the fight? If Max was thinking any of these thoughts, he was certainly right about one thing. Professional boxing was not one of Dean's major achievements. He knew that he could not disguise his true feelings, but he also knew that he could get through his next fights as a winner, and that was all that really mattered. He knew that he couldn't and wouldn't let down Max or Father Dillon. With that, Dean asked Max about the next fight.

"We're fighting the tenth ranked fighter in the welterweight division, a fighter by the name of Jose Zapata."

The name didn't mean much to Dean. He hadn't followed the fight scene as closely as Max and Father had, but he wanted to know more about his next opponent. Max told him that Jose had been in his gym several times and that on each occasion, Max had had an opportunity to watch him work out.

"Jose is technically a good boxer and a fair puncher. He's never been knocked out in his 18 professional fights. Being a southpaw, he will present some problems for you, but these can be worked out."

Dean listened carefully to each and every one of Max's comments. He knew that Max would not put him in with someone he could not defeat. His confidence in Max's ability as his trainer could not be challenged. As he had done so many times before, Dean would be an attentive student.

"We fight Jose in three weeks, so we have plenty to do before that fight."

As usual, Dean thanked Max, took a shower, dressed, and left the gym. Dean's daily routine didn't change very much. He still visited the Y, the hospital, the jail, the playground, Sam's bar, Father Dillon's library, and Max's gym. It was almost as if he was expected to make these visits. The funny thing about it all was that Dean enjoyed each of his stops. It was at one of these stops, the playground, that Dean met Sluice and his buddies. Sluice was the first to talk.

"I owe you an apology, Dino; my boys and me are sorry about that first meeting. We did it because we didn't want you to even meet the padre, but we were wrong about that too. Hopefully, you'll shake and forgive us. We've turned our lives around lately. Me and Jake are even thinking of asking Father Dillon to learn us to be altar boys like you. We'd have to go to church more often, and with some help from you or Father Dillon, we might learn about confession and other things. Max has already promised me that when I am ready that he will train and manage me in my fights. He said I have to first learn how to control my hatred. Seems a fighter has to be in control of his self. I plan to work hard on that. Maybe, Dean, you could also help me learn the fighting profession. I would be grateful."

Dean couldn't believe what was taking place. His

own hate had caused him to lash out at Sluice and his buddies, and here was Sluice asking for his help. It's a funny, strange place which we live in, thought Dean, but he smiled and told Sluice he would help. They left after Sluice shook Dean's outspread hand.

Here I am, an altar boy, and hopefully, a promising fighter, and I have already made some close friends. Funny how God works His ways? He certainly has turned my life around, and he has helped me know what I really want in life. Though he didn't openly pray or make the sign of the cross, Dean uttered quietly, "Thank you, Lord." Dean knew that he had a few more things to do: to win his next two fights, and to have that special meeting with Father Dillon.

After serving the Mass each morning and eating Mary's special fighter's breakfast, he would head for the gym. Max was always there to greet him.

"I want you to put on the gloves. I've lined up Jim to box against you for the next five or six days. With the exception of wrapping your hands, I want you to get use to fighting over six to twelve rounds. We'll work on your stamina. You'll have to be stronger, smarter, and in better shape than Jose."

With those comments, Max gave instructions to the two young fighters. Jim and Dean had become close friends. Each knew the other's weaknesses; each was technically a sound boxer. Jim's willingness to help his friend, Dean, prepare for the Zapata fight further strengthened their close friendship. If Dean won, Jim would have played an important part. The two touched gloves, smiled briefly, and went about their task. With both having youth and boxing skills, the rounds seem to go by like seconds on the clock. It seemed liked the two were still fighting the first round when Max blurted, "That's it, guys. Take off the gloves and hit the showers."

Dean and Jim climbed out of the ring and walked toward the showers. "Thanks, Jim; I'll never forget what you are doing for me."

Jim flashed a friendly smile, "Just win your next two fights. Who knows, you may end up being the champ, and I may end up being your opponent."

Dean pondered Jim's remarks. That would certainly be his biggest challenge. Dean couldn't even comprehend that particular fight. It could well happen because Jim, also trained by Max, was also making a record for himself. Regardless of what might happen, the two would always be friends. With that, Dean climbed into the shower stall. When he got back to St. Jude, he quietly opened the front door. Father Dillon heard the door close, and he entered the long narrow hallway which led to the upper and lower levels of the rectory.

"How'd it go?" asked the priest.

"We sort of had a mock fight, Jim and me. Max wants me to get use to going six to twelve rounds without getting tired. Max will increase the time each workout. I also plan to up my distance running to six to eight daily miles. I won't lose the fight by not being in shape."

Father Dillon smiled and patted Dean's shoulder. It was Thursday, and the fight was scheduled for Saturday night. The papers had already flashed headlines about the St. Jude altar boy moving up to fight a ranked fighter. Zapata was well-known by the boxing fans. The arena would be filled to capacity. Everyone would want to see this fight.

Father Dillon told Dean that he would be getting ten thousand dollars for fighting Zapata. Dean had never had more than a few bucks in his wallet. Now he would have to open a special bank account. Though he had never discussed percentages with Max or Father, he was prepared to give each twenty percent of his purse. It wasn't that much, but he knew each of them would be pleased with his gesture. He would cash the purse check, take out a saving account at the local bank, and ask for some blank checks so he could pay the two thousand to each of them. Dean thought about St. Jude, the badly needed kitchen, the appliances, and Mary. Win or lose, she could have those improvements. Fighting was becoming somewhat more interesting each passing day.

THE NIGHT OF the fight arrived, and the arena was jammed with people. Max moved his shield-covered hands, and Dean hit the targets as if he had a jack hammer in each fist. Hands wrapped, gloves on, Dean was more than ready to walk down the aisle to the ring. He would look quickly at the ringsiders before climbing into the ring.

He still remembered Max bellowing, "Focus, focus, jab, jab, and move." These had almost become sacred words in Dean's mind. Max wiped off Dean's sweating face, and put a clean, dry towel around his neck.

Father Dillon had a small rosary in his hands. He delicately touched each of the colored beads, made the Sign of the Cross with his right hand, and kissed gently the cross attached to the rosary. His deep and penetrating look at his altar boy told Dean how much this fight meant to the old priest.

Dean was ready; he would win this one for the two he cared most about. Both men followed Dean down the aisle to the ring apron. Max parted the ropes, and Dean stepped up and into the ring. Jose Zapata was already in the ring shadow boxing and moving in his corner.

The ring announcer introduced the two fighters. "In this corner, weighing 147 pounds, wearing the gold trunks and hailing from Minneapolis, Minnesota, with a record of one win with no losses, the challenger Dean Nelson. In this corner, weighing 147 pounds, wearing the black with gold trim trunks, the tenth-ranked welter weight, with a record of twelve wins and no losses with seven knockouts, hailing formerly from Mexico, now fighting out of Las Vegas, Nevada, Jose Zapata."

Dean didn't look over at Jose. He knew he would meet Zapata in the upcoming war. The referee motioned each fighter to the center of the ring. He made his comments to each of the fighters. "Touch gloves, and let's have a. clean fight."

With those words Dean walked slowly but deliberately to his corner. Max helped him remove his sweatshirt, took the towel from Dean's neck, and wiped his face gently. "Remember, stay focused, jab, jab, hit, and always keep moving. Don't stand flat-footed. Confidence, son," said Max.

Dean had never heard Max say "son" before, so it had a special meaning for him. He had considered Max and Father to be his two closest friends, but Max seemed to be saying something special to the young fighter. In all the weeks and months with Father and Max, Dean had never mentioned his father. Oh, he had said that he thought his father was living somewhere in Minneapolis, but he was even uncertain about that. If his father was still alive, he certainly had made no attempt to contact him. Max had never mentioned family either, so maybe the meeting of the two was much deeper than Dean had thought. It was something else that Dean would have to find out about Max. He knew that Father Dillon was probably his closest and dearest friend, but now Max's comment made him feel wanted. He liked the feeling. He had two special people who really cared for him. He would no longer have to search for the meaning of life, for friends. He was surrounded by the people who really cared.

Dean again noticed Mary, Sam, Dr. Browman, Addie and her new husband, Jeb, Jim, and Sluice and his friends. He wouldn't have to worry about fan support. He had his own rooting section.

The bell sounded; Dean and Jose touched gloves.

Dean noticed the determined look on Jose's face, but he was also determined. He flicked out two jabs that grazed Jose's chin, then quickly moved right from the southpaw, causing Jose's first jab to bounce off his left shoulder. The feeling out process was quite noticeable as each fighter jabbed and moved. The second and third rounds were about the same. Jabs from both fighters were common, and then, almost without Dean seeing it, Jose moved in closer and fired two punches to Dean's mid-section. Caught off balance for a moment, Dean dropped his elbows just a little, and Dean felt the first real punch of the fight. Jose was somewhat off balance, so the full force of the punch was not completely felt, but Dean knew that Jose had lethal power in both hands. He would stay at arms length and not allow Jose to get in close. The bell sounded ending the round and Dean went back to his corner.

Max spared few words: "Stay away from him. Don't allow him to get in close. He wants to hit your mid-section to slow you down, so he can get to you in the later rounds." Max wiped off Dean's face, gave him a shot of water, put Vaseline around his chin, cheeks, and forehead. The bell sounded.

Dean was somewhat faster than Jose. He was able to jab several times with both hands. Jose stopped short near the neutral corner, and Dean moved in with both hands digging into Jose's mid-section. A strange look crossed Jose's face, and Dean knew that he had hurt him. As Jose leaned slightly forward, Dean fired a left uppercut which caught Jose's chin. He fell backward, but he didn't go down as the round ended.

"You're getting to him," jawed Max. You've made him respect your punching power. He may come out more cautious, and if he does, move in, throw your combinations, and get out fast, always moving to your right. Whatever you do, don't go to your left, and never come straight back after throwing your punches. A lefty needs a big target to throw his big left hand."

Dean listened carefully to what Max was saying. The bell sounded for round six. Neither of the fighters was able to gain the upper hand, but Dean forced Jose into a corner again. He pounded both of his fists into Jose's mid-section, and again he was able to throw another uppercut which found its mark, but this time Jose managed to throw his left hand, and it caught Dean on his left cheek. Dean hurriedly covered up and moved out of trouble.

As he sat on his stool in his corner, Max hurriedly pressed a cold piece of steel to Dean's left cheek. The coldness would neutralize the swelling that was already beginning to show. A sip of water, and Dean was ready to battle. Round seven saw both fighters somewhat forget their boxing skills and found each of them pounding each other often. Dean heard Max shout above the yelling of the crowd, "Jab, jab and move." Dean heard and responded immediately as the round ended.

Max again wiped the sweat from Dean's face; he immediately applied the cold steel compressor to the swollen cheek. "You're doing fine, son. Just don't forget our fight plan."

Thus far, it had been a grueling fight for the two gladiators, but Dean had the strong feeling that he was in slightly better condition than Jose. He watched Jose get slowly off his stool as the bell sounded for round seven.

Jose was no longer on his toes and moving. He stood flat footed as he moved toward Dean. He remembered seeing the challenger in the fight Father Dillon was watching the night he had come to St. Jude. He, too, had come into the round flat footed, and the champ made him pay the price. Dean didn't have too much time to recall that fight, but he did know what happened to the challenger. He was ready for Jose's charge. He blocked both of Jose's punches and pounded his right and left squarely on Jose's chest and chin. Jose's gloved hands unexpectedly dropped, no longer protecting his chin and face, and Dean fired a combination to those unprotected areas. Jose tried desperately to clinch, but Dean would have no part of that. He must have hit Jose a dozen times before Jose was able to clinch and tie Dean up.

Max and Father Dillon had smiles on their faces. "He's all yours," whispered Max into Dean's ear. Don't let up; you hurt him and he's getting tired. If you finish the next round as you did the last, the fight may be all over. Jab, jab and move, and if he drops his hands again, hit him with that straight right. Are you tired?"

"No sir," Dean blurted. The next round was all

Dean. Jose had to take a knee in order to stop the beating he was taking. The referee counted to eight as the bell rang, and Jose walked awkwardly to his corner. Dean hadn't noticed, but two huge, swollen bumps appeared under Jose's eyes. His nose was still bleeding when round nine began.

Dean fired six straight jabs into Jose's nose and face. There were no return punches as Dean darted in and out of Jose's reach. Another flurry of Dean's punches; blood smeared all over Jose's arms and chest. A white towel was tossed into the ring. Jose's corner had seen enough; the fight was over. Dean had never been a showboat fighter, but this time he raised both of his arms in a sign of victory.

The crowd was on its feet, roaring and yelling their approvals. Before going back to his corner, Dean wrapped his arm around Jose's neck and shoulders, and he whispered something into Jose's ear. He would later tell Max that he had told Jose he was a terrific fighter. Dean's gesture brought another roar from the crowd. Dean sat on his stool as Max unlaced his gloves, wiped his face, and gave him a fatherly hug. Father Dillon quickly entered the ring. "I knew you had it in you," the priest said softly. He, too, gave Dean a friendly pat on the head.

The ring announcer announced the winner. "Are you ready for a title fight?" yelled the fight's radio announcer.

Dean looked but chose not to answer the question. "Ask my manager and my trainer," was all Dean said.

The crowd was still standing, still cheering the now famous altar boy. He saw the faces and the smiles of all of his closest friends, especially Jim, who had been his most important sparring partner the past few weeks. Jim, much like Sluice had done at the first fight, flashed his fingers in a victory salute. The friendship between the two younger men was securely knotted.

FATHER DILLON HAD Dean's ten thousand dollar check, and he smiled as he presented it to Dean.

"Twenty percent is yours, Father, and twenty percent goes to Max. My portion will help you to refinish Mary's kitchen, and it should be enough to get a new stove, refrigerator, and dishwasher. Mary deserves the attention." With that, Dean tucked the check into his wallet. "I plan to get a savings account in town tomorrow, and hopefully the bank can give me two blank checks for Max and you."

Dean had a huge grin on his face after making those comments. He thought about Father, Jim, and Max. "How lucky can one person be?" thought the young altar boy. Just months ago, he was being beaten and kicked by a now close friend, Sluice.

He knelt down by his bed and said the Our Father prayer for the very first time. He had plenty to think about: his fights, his many friends, and the One Person who had made all of this possible, his God. Dean had never felt this way until now. He still had something special to discuss with Father Dillon, but for now that could wait. He climbed into bed a very different person.

The next morning, Dean journeyed to the local bank, took out a savings account, asked for a few blank checks, signed the ten thousand dollar check, and gave it to the bank teller.

"We appreciate your business," said the bank teller. "Aren't you that altar boy fighter from St. Jude?"

Dean flashed a quick, "You betcha, man," picked up his checks, and headed for home. He wrote the first check for two thousand dollars to Father James Dillon; another was made out for two thousand dollars to Max Lender. Two of his dearest friends would now realize how he felt about them. Then he completed another five hundred dollar check to pay Dr. Browman. He would buy Jeb Stuart a special present. He found out from Father Dillon that Jeb enjoyed fishing. Dean would buy Jeb a rod and reel. For a few moments, Dean felt just a little like Santa Claus; it was a real Christmas for the young lad.

Dean couldn't wait to visit the gym and Max. He stepped into the gym and Max greeted him.

"You're early; we don't have a workout for a least another two hours."

"I have a present for you, Max. Thought I would come by a little early. I've got two other stops to make before I return. Here, Max, it isn't much, but it'll show you how much I have appreciated your coaching and your teaching."

Dean didn't know whether he should ask Max about the "son" bit, but he could do that some other time.

Max looked down at the check, clearly signed by Dean Nelson. He wanted to fix up his place so it would look better when the media stopped by. This certainly would be more than enough to trim up the place.

"Thanks, son," was all that Max could say. He flashed a quick smile and gently patted Dean's shoulder. "See you here in a few hours." Dean couldn't help but remember that Max had used the "son" word once more.

Dean's next stop was at Dr. Browman's house. Though he had seen the doctor at his last two fights, he had not had time to talk with him. This would be another special visit. Dean knocked on the doctor's door. Dr. Browman opened it and saw Dean standing on his small porch.

"I've got something for you, Dr. Browman, something which I said I would give to you if I ever found a good paying job." Dean handed the five hundred dollar check to the old doctor.

Dr. Browman didn't know just what to say. "I have attended to a lot of people, both the young and the old. Some said, 'Thank you', but others just seemed to turn away. You're a very special young person, Dean. I hope you stay a long time with the Padre. He and Max love you as if you were part of their families." The two shook hands and Dean turned and left.

It was getting late; he wouldn't have time to buy Jeb's fishing gifts so he hurriedly headed for Max's gym.

Seventeen

Max's Boxing Career

"**One more warm** up fight and we may be given a contract to fight the champ," said Max. He saw the sparkle appear in Dean's eyes when he made that statement. Everything seemed to be going much too fast for Dean, but he was enjoying the roller coaster ride.

Dean put on his trunks, sweat shirt, and his shoes. Max was waiting for him in the gym. "Our training tactics will be somewhat the same, but I want you to work the speed bag and the ropes harder than ever before. I know that you run six to eight miles daily, but I want you to do more speed work than before. I want the legs and calves especially strong. Our championship fight may be only weeks away, and endurance will be a major factor. You'll probably be looking at fifteen rounds, and our training has only been for ten to twelve rounds, so we have still a lot of hard work ahead of us." With those comments, Max left Dean and went into his office.

Dean didn't need to be told to commence with his training. Like a kid on a playground, he began jumping rope. As he worked out, Dean looked into Max's office. He could see through the upper glass door that Max was on the phone. Max was probably talking with Father Dillon about the next fight. Dean felt that this might be the right time to ask Max about the "son" comment. He knocked on the door, and Max motioned him to come in.

"Could we have a short talk," asked Dean.

"Why certainly, son, what's on your mind?" asked Max.

"You remember the last fight? Well, when I was in the corner between rounds you made a comment, like 'You're doing real good, son.' Do you remember saying that?"

"Yup," replied Max.

"I had never asked you about your family, about marriage, or your prize fighting career, and I have never heard you mention your father, your mother, any brothers or sisters, etc."

"I don't say much about me and my family. Both of my parents are dead; I have one brother, and I haven't heard from him in years, but funny, the other day I got a postcard from him. He evidently is reading the sport news and he must have heard or seen something mentioning the 'altar boy fighter.' It's been all over the news. The papers even mentioned me and the padre.

It's like we all are celebrities. Calling you son was no accident. I've never had much time for women and thus. I have never been married, but if I had, I would like to have had a son like you. I know that we have only been together just a few months, but I can't help but say that I think of you as my son and not a distant prize fighter. Oh, I'm pleased that you like the fight game. I can't deny that, but I can also say that when you are in the ring, I would like to protect you as a father might want to. That's why I'm always telling you the things which will keep you from getting hurt in the ring. If anything serious happens to you, I would consider it my fault. I hope you don't mind that I feel as I do?

"About my boxing career, I started or got interested in boxing at the age of fifteen. I lived in a very tough neighborhood, so fighting was part of my daily life. We had a beat-up gym in the neighborhood, and most of the kids frequented the place. In some ways, it was much like my present gym, but our equipment was old and worn. The place did allow us to get off the streets. I just loved to punch the bags. It allowed me to forget about my problems at home and in school. Wasn't long, and I decided to make boxing my career. I quit school, and I concentrated on my boxing. Had some seventy amateur fights. I mostly fought as a welter weight like you, but I also fought as a middle weight. Luck was with me, and I won our district's golden glove tournament. I advanced to the finals of the golden glove tournament in Detroit. My final fight was against a welter weight from Chicago. He was three years older than me, and that turned out to be the difference. His experience paid off, and I lost the bout. I had trouble getting a job because I wasn't a high school graduate, but I found enough odd jobs to pay my room and board. I turned pro when I was nineteen. I still frequented the gym in my neighborhood and the owner, Abe Painter, a former boxer, agreed to manage and train me. I wish that I could say that I had fought for the championship as a welter, but that just never happened to me. I had over fifty fights and won more than I lost. Was never knocked off my feet, and I fought some of the top contenders of my time. My biggest problem was moving up the ladder so I might get a shot at the champ, but each time that I would fight a contender, I would lose by a decision or by a TKO. I made enough from boxing to keep me going. My manager knew and liked me, so at the age of thirty-five I put the gloves away. Abe said he would give me a low interest loan if I decided to buy a gym or go into some other business. You know the rest. I now own my place, and your success certainly isn't hurting my business. With Sluice and other paying prospects using my facilities, I, too, am on the road to success." With that, he turned back to some work on his desk.

Dean left Max's office, but he now was convinced beyond a doubt that Max and Father Dillon were two very special people. He wasn't about to let either down. Dean went back to working the speed bag. It wasn't long after when Max joined Dean.

"Well, son, your next fight will be against Chuck Maxim. Ranked sixth in the welter weight division,

Chuck will be a formidable opponent. Though he had never worked out in my gym, I did see his last two fights. Two ten-rounders, and he went the distance both times, winning both with unanimous decisions. He had a long career as an amateur, and he has had over twenty professional bouts. His record includes eighteen wins, five knockouts, and two losses. The two losses were to ranked fighters. As far as I know, Chuck has never been on the canvas. He's not a big puncher, but he's smart. He is always in good shape, technically sound, with a very pleasing personality. He'll come prepared. This won't be an easy fight, but it should not be a brutal battle. Chuck's a clean boxer; he won't brawl with you, and he will avoid accidental head butts. He's never been cut nor has he had any serious injuries. I expect a clean, hard fought fight. Any questions?"

"Whatever you say; you know fighters; you know me and my skills. I'll look forward to meeting Maxim." With that, Dean went about his workout.

After showering, Dean decided to go to the mall and buy Jeb's gift. He would have Father drive him to Jeb's house. Dean stepped into one of the larger sport stores in the city. He had done some fishing as a boy, so fishing gear wasn't something that he didn't know about. He looked down the aisles of fishing rods. He wanted to get a six foot or longer rod, and he planned to get a closed-face Garcia reel. It didn't take long for Dean to find exactly what he was looking for. The reel and rod cost close to a hundred dollars, but it was one of the better units. He knew Jeb would be pleased with his choice. When he got back to his room, he told Father Dillon about Jeb's gifts, and Father agreed to drive him to Jeb's house. Later, the two pulled into Jeb's driveway. Dean got out, knocked on Jeb's door, and Jeb greeted him.

"Can't stay long, Mr. Stuart, but I have a gift for you for driving me to Dr. Browman's and for dropping me off at Father's house." Jeb took the gift and thanked Dean.

"Sure you can't stay awhile?" asked Jeb.

"Wish I could, but Father has some parishioners visiting this evening, so I better ride back. Thanks anyway." He would ask Jeb some other time how he liked his gift.

Eighteen

A Formidable Foe

Dean kneeled down beside his bed. He made the sign of the cross and softly prayed. "Thank you, dear Lord, for having put Max Lender, Jeb Stuart, and Father Dillon into my life. Just a few months ago, I was a homeless kid not even knowing where my next meal would come from. Like the Star, You have directed me to these three wise men." He said a few more prayers, blessed himself, and climbed into bed.

Dean's days serving daily Mass were always meaningful. After each Mass, he would frequent Father's office, and the priest and Dean would discuss many varied topics. He now fully understood the Mass, the confessional, even something as complex as the Trinity. Father Dillon did not seem to understand why Dean kept asking questions about the Catholic rituals. Dean would only smile and thank Father for taking the time to respond to his many questions. Just two more fights and Dean would ask the old priest to have that special meeting. It was only a matter of time, thought Dean.

The days passed by, and Dean continued his chores and his training. Max had lined up a number of sparring partners, each with a different but special skill. Though Dean had not had many fights, each day in Max's gym brought him new and meaningful experiences. It was almost like each new sparring partner was another fight in Dean's short career. Father Dillon, making his daily visits, stopped at the gym. Dean saw the priest in Max's office. He assumed that the two were discussing the fight. The office door opened, and Father came over to the ring.

"Dean, you're going to get thirty-five thousand to fight Maxim. If it's all right with you, I'll get the contract signed."

Dean yelled, "Yippee," and continued with his work in the ring. Father made a few more remarks to Max, and then he left the gym.

"We fight Maxim in five days. I would suggest that you don't do any additional miles the next few days. Allow your legs to rest. The same will be true with your ring workouts. I'm going to cut back on those. No more sparring partners. Do some shadow boxing and your floor exercises. I want you fresh when you climb into the ring against Maxim," were Max's final remarks.

The local papers were called, and the sport headlines were: "Altar boy Dean Nelson fights Chuck Maxim." Fans knew Maxim. They knew he was another ranked fighter. They knew that this would be Dean's biggest bout. Prior to the fight, St. Jude was literally filled with reporters who wanted to get more pictures of this altar boy prize fighter. A picture with Father Dillon's arm looped over Dean's shoulder appeared in the sport section of the Daily News. The story read: "Fr. Dillon, manager of Dean Nelson, signs the contract to fight Chuck Maxim."

The next few days, St. Jude was crowded before and after the daily morning Mass. Dean and the padre were celebrities. The flash bulb cameras took numerous pictures of the promising newcomer. Dean liked the attention, but he also knew that this new-found fame would be short lived. He had other plans, and prize fighting would not be a part of them, but for now, Dean enjoyed what he was currently doing.

The night of the Maxim fight was just hours away. Dean had knelt quietly by his bed the night before the Maxim fight. He made the sign of the cross, slowly touching his forehead, his chest, his two shoulders, and then pressing together his hands.

"Please, dear Lord, give me the strength to win this fight. Also, dear Lord, bless Max and Father Dillon for all their efforts in training and teaching me to be a better fighter, and most importantly, being a better person. Without their love and understanding, I would still be walking the streets, hitch hiking the highways, and wondering about life's meaning. These two men have opened up my life. Each has accepted me as a person and a friend. Thank you, dear Lord." Dean felt something special inside; he knew he would have another successful evening.

MAX GAVE DEAN his final instructions. "Box him the first round, be focused, keep your chin tucked in. Remember to jab and move, jab and move." Dean had heard those words so many times in the last few months, but he also realized the importance of what Max was saying. Concentration was an art in itself. Dean would have to focus on the fight. He could not allow his thoughts to focus on some of his other important things.

The announcer's voice broke the silence which had engulfed Dean. "In this corner, wearing red shorts, from Minneapolis, Minnesota, weighing in at 147 pounds, with a record of two wins and no losses, the up and coming Dean Nelson, and in this corner, wearing the black trunks, weighing in at 146, with a record of twelve wins and no losses and having scored six knockouts, fighting out of Salt Lake City, Utah, Chuck Maxim."

The referee motioned each fighter to the center of the ring for his final instructions. "I want a clean fight. Touch gloves, and let's get on with the fight."

The bell sounded for round one. Dean moved and jabbed; Chuck did the same. Both fighters were obviously trying to size up their opponents. Dean fired two more jabs, and one caught the edge of Maxim's chin. He moved away and covered up. Dean moved in again and this time was able to get three quick jabs at the moving target. Chuck stopped short and fired his own jabs. Dean caught two of them on his arm. The round ended. Rounds two and three were fought much the same way.

"You have to bring down his arms; you've got to fire at his mid-section. Chuck's keeping his elbows in tight and his gloves close to his face. Pound him below his elbows. That may cause him to drop his gloves so that you can get a straight right hand at the open chin. Be careful; don't throw your right unless he brings those gloves down."

The bell sounded for round four, and Dean went immediately to the center of the ring. Chuck was carrying his gloves high, so Dean fired a left and right to Chuck's mid-section. Chuck wasn't expecting these punches. Instead of moving away, he stood his ground and at the same time dropped his gloves from his face and chin. Dean saw the opportunity that Max had talked about. He threw a hard straight right to Chuck's chin. The punch flashed sweat from Chuck's mouth. The crowd went wild. Chuck's knees buckled a little, but he didn't go down. Instead, he began to back pedal and moved away from Dean. Dean wasn't about to let him get out of his range. He knew that he had hurt Chuck with his right hand. He hoped to do the same with his left hand. Chuck cleared his head and fought back. He fired a number of jabs at Dean, but again, these hit Dean's arms and caused no damage. Chuck had a different look on his face. He realized that this altar boy fighter was for real. He couldn't make anymore mistakes. The bell sounded ending the fourth round.

Max was quick to wipe off Dean's face; he gave Dean the water bottle. "How do you feel, son," Max whispered.

"I'm just fine, feel great," was Dean's quick reply.

"Keep hitting that mid-section. Chuck may give you another chance to score your right again."

Rounds five and six were basically standoffs. Neither fighter scored enough clean punches to win the rounds. Dean sat patiently in his corner as Max again mentioned going to Chuck's mid-section. In round six, Dean noticed that Chuck's jabs seemed to be slower and lighter. He also had watched Chuck's corner work on Chuck's face. He noticed a slight swelling under Chuck's left eye. It wasn't much to go on, but Dean felt that he could concentrate his jabs into that area, and in round seven, Dean found his mark. He fired a series of straight right jabs at the swollen area. Chuck brought up his gloves to protect his chin and face, and Dean immediately pounded two straight lefts to Chuck's mid-section. He knew he had hurt Chuck with those two punches. Chuck moved in and forced the first clinch of the fight. The referee separated the fighters as the bell sounded.

Dean hurried to his corner. "Great round," barked Max. "You hurt him with those two straight lefts. He's boxing defensively now, so you've got to stay on him. Don't even give him air to breathe. Also, pound with your jabs at the swollen cheek. It's beginning to affect his vision. Don't let up now. Jab, punch, and move. Don't ever stop moving. How are your legs?"

"Great!" was Dean's only response. Max knew that the rope jumping and the added speed work had greatly added to Dean's overall endurance. Dean was controlling the fight. Just a few more rounds and Dean might be looking at another TKO. Max didn't tell Dean this, but his years of experience made Max feel this way. He had a fighter who listened, who learned, and who performed. He knew that he had the new welterweight champion of the world. With a slight smile, Max gave Dean some additional instructions and round eight began.

Chuck held his gloves high to protect his swollen face. Dean moved in closer to make his jabs more effective. He hit Chuck with six straight jabs, and Chuck moved from the center of the ring to a neutral corner. Chuck was flicking with his glove to his eye and chin. Dean hadn't seen it before, but Chuck had a slight cut just above his eye. Blood trickled slowly into Chuck's eye. It wasn't a fight stopping cut, but it was bothering Chuck, so Dean began to fire his jabs into the injured area. The cut became bigger and more blood found its way to Chuck's eye. Almost as if by instinct, Dean noticed that Chuck had brought both of his gloves up to protect the eye and chin areas. A left and right hand found Chuck's mid-section, and Chuck was hurt. He threw two or three weak jabs, but these had no effect upon Dean. Dean pounded two more lefts to the rib section. Chuck tried to clinch, but Dean moved quickly away. The bell ended the round.

Max's comments were clear. "Keep jabbing that swollen area and that cut eye. When he pulls up his gloves to cover his chin and the cut, don't hesitate; go downstairs. You've got him, son. Unless I miss my guess, he will go down in this round. Be cautious; don't make any stupid mistakes. Remember, a hurt fighter can be a dangerous fighter." Max splashed Dean's face, wiped off the excess water, and allowed Dean a small sip of water as the ninth round began.

Chuck had a strange look on his face, and Dean sensed that this would be the round. He did everything just the way he had been trained to do. Jab and move, jab and move. Half way into the round, Dean managed to force Chuck into a corner, the first time in the fight. He moved in, firing jab after jab, and Chuck was no longer able to protect the swollen, cut areas. As he had done in the previous round, Chuck brought up his gloves even higher to protect his injured areas. His elbows no longer protected his mid-section, and Dean moved in throwing two vicious lefts to Chuck's rib area. Chuck made no effort to clinch, but instead, he went down on one knee with blood trickling down his face and chin. The referee had reached the count of eight, and Chuck had made no move to continue the fight. It was over; Dean had scored his first knockout. Before going to his corner, Dean put his arm around Chuck's neck and whispered, "Good fight." The audience reacted to Dean's gesture with a standing ovation. Dean realized that possibly one more fight would help him to realize Father Dillon's dream. Time was on his side, but Dean was also looking ahead to his future, to his own dream. He hadn't told anyone about it, but he would soon.

Max was the first to hug his young fighter. "You did it, son; you're on your way to a title shot."

Father Dillon also climbed into the ring. "You were something else!" said the padre. "You were never flatfooted; you were never tired; and you were always focused. Won't be long and you may very well be the new welterweight champion of the world." Dean grinned when he heard those words. He knew that Father's dream might just happen.

The next few days at St. Jude were busy ones. Sport reporters with cameras literally stormed the church with one intention. They wanted to get pictures of Dean and Father Dillon, and both responded willingly. Father Dillon realized that the publicity wouldn't hurt St. Jude, and it certainly wouldn't hurt Dean's growing popularity. Both Father and Dean were interviewed. One reporter could be heard asking the priest if he had any plans for a championship bout. Father Dillon simply replied, "We'll have to wait and see. We'll have to consult with Dean's trainer, Max Fender. You might want to talk with him. He knows better than me about Dean's condition, about his progress, and about his next fight." The reporter thanked the priest and left.

Within days after his last fight, Dean was still going about with his daily and weekly routines. He continued to serve the morning Mass. He found time to help

Mary with some of the chores around the church, and he continued to go with Father Dillon to visit the sick, the needy, and the dying. Of all of their visits, Dean found their visits to the sick and to the dying most rewarding. He hoped that in some small ways he was helping them. In fact, Dean would visit many patients who were not on Father Dillon's list. He would ask the nurses if any new patients without strong family ties had been recently admitted. One special female patient was Stella Abrams. She was in her late twenties or early thirties. Like many of the patients in the intensive ward, Stella had cancer. She had already gone through weeks of radiation and chemotherapy. A scarf shielded her hair line. Dean had introduced himself as a friend of Father Dillon, and he had told her he would like to visit with her each time that they came to the hospital. Stella's smile indicated that she would like his visits, and so their friendship grew. Stella knew that she was dying and that the pain pills made it possible for her to be somewhat comfortable. During his most recent visit, Stella had asked Dean if he would hold her hand and sit with her for a little while. Dean took Stella's outstretched hand. The moment their hands touched, Dean realized the importance of his visits to the hospital. Though he did not fully understand the impact which his visits had on Stella, he would always note how peaceful and comfortable she looked as he sat by her hospital bedside holding her hand. This was still another experience Dean had never had before. He gently tapped Stella's shoulder. She opened her eyes, looked softly and smiled at Dean. She made a feeble gesture with her hand, a thank you for his timely visit. Dean left the hospital with Father Dillon.

At first he had little or nothing to say to the priest, but then in a breaking voice, Dean asked, "Father, why must people suffer before God takes them?"

Father Dillon looked carefully and deliberately at Dean. "God has his own special ways in preparing his followers to enter the Gates of Heaven. You may or may not remember that when the Lord was being crucified that He also said, 'Father, why have you forsaken me?' The Lord also suffered and died for all of us. Your visits with Stella, and Stella's worsened condition are all a part of God's Plan."

Though Dean didn't understand fully what Father was trying to convey to him, he did realize that God was very much with Stella and was watching over her. He also felt that maybe God was the person who brought him to visit the sick and the dying. This last thought brought greater meaning to Dean. There would be other visits, other revelations.

Nineteen

A Non-Title Fight

HAVING FINISHED AT the hospital, Dean was ready to go to Max's gym for his afternoon workout. Max, flashing a broad smile, was waiting for him.

"I figured that you would be by today. Got some special news which might interest you. Got a call from the welterweight champion's owner-manager. He wants to know if we would consider a non-title fight. He feels that it would be a huge draw, and he is willing to set up the match with you getting $100,000 for the fight."

Bob Fitzgerald had just won the title from the former title holder, Randy Batch, but the fight had been close through the twelve rounds. Max was thinking that Fitzgerald's manager was probably looking for a warm up fight before giving Batch a return match. Dean was quick to respond.

"You know me, Max. If you think I can give the

champ a good fight, and if you feel I am good enough to stay with the champ, I say we take the fight. It will bring us closer to a possible title shot ourselves."

With that comment, Dean went about his workout. Max knew that Dean depended upon him to make the final decision to okay the fight. Max also knew that Dean's workouts had to be carefully planned. There was plenty to do to prepare Dean for the likes of the champ, Fitzgerald. Max would get a film copy of Fitzgerald's championship fight. He would study it carefully before having Dean watch the film. Hundred of things were going through Max's head, but he knew one thing. He wasn't about to let Dean, his son, go into any ring unprepared. His keen eyes would study Fitzgerald's every move, and he would relay to Dean what had to be done to stay close or possibly win the match.

DEAN KNELT DOWN by his bed. He made the sign of the cross and uttered, "Please, dear Lord, give me the strength and the courage to fight and possibly to win this next fight. Lord, Father Dillon had a special dream when he was a young fighter. Please, dear Lord, let me help Father realize that dream, and if you can, dear Lord, watch over me. Don't allow me to get hurt so badly that I wouldn't be able to fight that championship match. I know, Lord, that I am asking for a lot, but Max and Father Dillon have given me a new look at life, and You, Lord, are a part of it."

With those final words, Dean made the sign of the cross a second time, and then he slipped quietly into his bed. It wasn't too long before Dean's deep sleep included a very special dream.

Dean was up early the next morning. He made his bed, showered, and headed for the church. Father Dillon, with a smile on his face, greeted Dean.

"Max called me shortly after you came home from your daily workout. He told me about the Bob Fitzgerald fight and that you had confidence in his decision to fight Fitzgerald. I am very proud of you, Dean, and I know that you will give Fitzgerald a great fight. Why, you might even win it!"

With those words Father Dillon turned and walked slowly to the altar. Though Dean had served at the Masses for many weeks, he felt something special about this Mass. Just before reading the Gospel, the priest turned to those parishioners attending the Mass. Lately the church was filled with bowed heads.

"I want all of you to know that my altar boy, Dean, has accepted a non-title fight with the welterweight champion of the world, Bob Fitzgerald. The fight will be scheduled some five weeks from today. If you can, Dean, Max, and I would like you to attend. More importantly, I ask all of you to say some special prayers for Dean so that he goes into and comes out of the fight unhurt. I know that this is a strange request coming from the altar of St. Jude, but I am sure that the Lord will understand and forgive me for making this request. Father Dillon read the gospel and continued with the Mass.

Dean had a keen feeling. He was ready to have Father Dillon hear his first confession, so he could also take part in Communion with the other parishioners. After the Mass ended, Father and Dean walked into the sacristy and removed their church garments. Dean was the first to speak.

"Father, when you have time, I would like to make my confession, so I can also partake of the Body and Blood of Christ. If it is possible, I would like to receive Communion each time that I serve the Mass."

Father Dillon looked carefully at Dean. "I was hoping that you would soon make your confession and would become a regular communicant. At that time, another of my dreams would become a reality. If you would like a few days to prepare, I will hear your confession later in the week."

Dean thanked Father Dillon and told the priest that he would be ready on Friday. Again he thanked him, left the sacristy, and went into the house. Mary was already preparing breakfast for the two men.

"I understand that you're planning to fight again," Mary said. "If you plan on fighting a champion of the world, you are going to have to eat and drink special foods and fluids. I've never served a challenger before, but there is always a first time for everything. I would imagine that you must also watch your weight closely if you wish to be successful."

Mary's smile indicated that she would meet the

challenge and that she would prepare the proper foods for an up and coming young fighter. She kind of enjoyed that she would be a part of what she had heard Dean utter so softly, his dream. She didn't know what that dream really was about, but that didn't matter. She could feel the changes which had come over the old priest, and these changes were good ones.

Dean and Father Dillon finished their breakfasts and proceeded to their daily visits. When they returned to St. Jude, Dean walked slowly into his room. Kneeling by his bed, he gave careful thought to what he would say at his first confession with Father Dillon. He had studied the confession pamphlet. He knew that he would have to indicate when he had his last confession; he would have to think carefully about what sins he had committed. Dean was ready for his first confession. He would fully understand Father Dillon's possible questions, his advice, and his penance. Two days passed and then it was Friday.

The two participated in the Mass, had their usual breakfast, and then Father said rather deliberately, "Would you like to go back into the church, Dean, and I'll hear your confession?"

Dean didn't have to be asked twice. He nodded his head and followed the elderly priest to the confessional. Father Dillon was the first to enter and Dean followed. He knelt on the carpeted pew and looked at the little closed door. The little door opened, and Dean could see his friend, his priest.

"Bless me, Father, for I have sinned." Dean uttered the words slowly and devoutly. "Father, I can't remember when I made my last confession, but it was many years ago. I have given careful thought to the sins that I have committed, but again, I cannot say with accuracy the number of times I committed each one."

Father made it easier for Dean by saying, "Just mention briefly the sins and the reasons for committing them."

Dean talked about not going to Mass, about not making his Easter duty, about talking back to his drunken father, about failing to listen to his mother's complaints, and about swearing profanely when angered. He ended by telling the priest about the gang beating that Sluice and his buddies gave him when he was hitch hiking and how he wanted someday to get even with Sluice and the others for that beating. He mentioned how he had hit Sluice on the playground and that he wanted to hurt him badly for what he had said to the priest. The confession took over an hour.

When he had finished, Dean listened carefully and thoughtfully to what the priest had to say.

"Dean, my son, you have encountered sins which are very much a part of everyone's life. Christ knows that at times men and women will become angry, that they will not always be in control of their minds or their bodies. On our daily tours, you have witnessed both the good and the bad, but even some of the things considered bad can be turned around and become good. Look what has happened to Sluice and his buddies. Why, they are altar boys; they attend your fights; Sluice wants to be a prize fighter like you. A lot of things which we consider sins turn out to be God's blessings, but I have said enough. For your penance, I want you to receive Communion daily; I want you to pray daily, at least twenty minutes, for the less fortunate in our society, and I want you to work strenuously with Max in preparation for your next fight. I want you to win."

The little confessional door closed, and Dean continued to kneel quietly in the confessional. He thought carefully about what he had confessed; he thought about his penance; then he thought about something he had not told the old priest. It wasn't that he was lying, but it just wasn't the time to tell Father Dillon his most precious thoughts. That would come at another confession; that would come after Father's dream had been realized.

Dean made the sign of the cross ever so slowly. He would receive Communion the next morning. He wondered about the Body and Blood of the Christ. He was embarking on another phase of his new life.

Dean knelt at the foot of his bed. His prayers were to be special this particular evening. He began by thanking God for bringing him to Father's home, for allowing him to make many friends, specifically those at the hospital, and especially Father Dillon, Max, Mary, and Sluice. Then Dean focused on his penance to pray for the unfortunates. He thought about the homeless; he thought about the suffering and the dying, about Stella, and about the countless numbers who had little or no faith. He also asked the Lord to guide and watch over him in his prize-fighting endeavors. He realized that there were limitations even in his prayers. With that, Dean softly touched his forehead, his two shoulders and his heart, uncupped his hands, and crawled slowly into bed. He would have many special dreams this particular evening, and having Communion the next day would fulfill a most coveted dream.

Dean was up early the next morning. He greeted Mary; he saw Father Dillon headed for the sacristy; he hurried to catch up to the priest.

"Why, you're in a big hurry this morning. Do you have something special on your mind?"

Dean didn't respond; he knew Father understood why he felt the way he did.

The Mass began as it usually did. Dean brought Father the water and the wine. Though this was not a special church day, the church was again filled to capacity. The media, especially, held seats in the first few pews, and cameras were in visible sight. Father had not prohibited camera use, but it was beginning to be a distraction.

The Mass continued. The priest bowed his head while holding the chalice in his hands. Dean got the communion plate; he held it under each of the parishioners' chins, and then he followed the priest back to the altar stairs. He knelt on the bottom step; Father noticed that Dean was holding the plate under his chin; the priest selected one of the holy wafers and placed it gently on Dean's tongue. With his eyes closed, Dean bowed his head slowly; he consumed what was now the Body and Blood of Christ. Something strange seemed to come over him. He felt something he had never felt before. He now realized why Father always closed his eyes and bowed his head when he was holding his most holy vessel.

A flash of light from a reporter's camera brought Dean back into the real world. A reporter had taken a picture of this very special moment. Father had also seen the flashes, and he slowly turned to those in attendance.

"I know that you are simply doing your jobs, but I would like all of you to remember that this is God's House, so I am asking that from here on that you refrain from taking pictures during the Holy Mass. With that, Dean and Father left the altar and made their way to the sacristy. Dean expected Father to make some special comments, but instead, he simply said, "Mary's waiting breakfast for us."

After breakfast, Dean said that he was going to the gym to watch films of Fitzgerald's last fight. Father was welcomed to join Dean and Max. He accepted the request, and he drove Dean to the gym.

Max had his projector and screen set up. In fact, Max had scanned the film several times. He had made a pad of notes that he would relay to Dean and the priest. Max had always enjoyed Father's friendship. The two had obviously talked with each other about their prize fighting days. Father might also see something Dean might not see and give him special tips. Max pressed the "on" switch of the projector, and the three viewed the first round.

"Did you notice anything in that round?" asked Max.

Dean responded, "Fitzgerald moves his legs well, and he has exceptional head movement. I especially noticed that all of his punches began with straight jabs, and he never went straight back when Batch countered. It's just like what you've been telling me during my past fights."

The three studied each of the rounds carefully. In the fourth round, Fitzgerald threw an overhand right to the jaw and fired two straight lefts to Batch's midsection.

Father was the first to say, "He's got a great right hand, and he follows up with his left hand. He's not a single hand puncher, and that makes him even more dangerous."

Dean listened and watched carefully. He had Max

run round four several times. The three watched, discussed, and pointed out Fitzgerald's tendencies, his strengths, and his weaknesses. There weren't very many weaknesses. Max made special references to rounds eight, nine, and ten. It was in these rounds that Batch slowed his movements and his punches. Batch clinched more often, and Max noticed that Fitzgerald would pound his fists into Batch's mid-section on each break. Fitzgerald knew that he was slowing Batch down with his body shots.

Dean knew that Fitzgerald, probably in the sixth, seventh, and eighth rounds, would try to do the same thing to him. He watched these rounds repeatedly. He would try to prevent Fitzgerald from doing the same to him. He also knew that Max would be throwing the heavy ball into his midsection at each of the workouts. Dean would also increase his time doing sit ups to strengthen his mid-section.

In the eleventh round Batch got caught with a straight right hand to his right eyebrow. The force of the punch opened a slight cut. Batch's cut man closed the wound, but Fitzgerald pounded away at it in the twelfth and final round.

"If you get a cut, Dean, you can count on Fitzgerald targeting it," Father commented.

Dean had never been cut in any of his previous fights, but he did have the scarred lip that he got in the beating from Sluice and his gang. He might have to protect that area, but that injury would not impair his eyesight like it did for Batch. Max mentioned that they would watch the film again but told Dean to continue his rope jumping, shadow boxing, weight lifting, pushups, punching bag, and also the big bag.

"I have three sparring partners that will be with us for the next few weeks. I'm gonna have a lightweight, a welterweight, and a middleweight work with you. The lightweight will provide you with added speed; the welterweight with equal speed and weight, and the middleweight with heavier punching power. When you can keep comfortable with all three, you'll be ready for Fitzgerald.

"We may also fine tune some of your other skills, including going to the body, uppercuts, and punishing straight right and left punches. Also, spend several minutes each day shadow boxing. Look carefully into the mirror; watch when and where you carry your hands after each punch. I want that chin tucked in and the elbows protecting your mid-section. A good fighter will pound that mid-section in an effort to get you to drop your hands. A great fighter will catch you consistently if you become careless with your defense."

A Non-Title Fight

Dean knew what Max and Father were trying to convey to him. It was not something that went into one ear and out of the other. He was a careful listener, not only to tips in boxing, but he listened religiously to comments made by Father Dillon while saying Mass, while preaching the gospel, and while speaking to hospital patients and to others. Everything said carried some meaning for this young man; Dean worshiped Max. He would not let Max or Father down. Though Max had not told him, Dean upped his daily running to eight miles, and he always finished his running workout with sprints. He wanted to be in the best shape of his life. He also knew that the ability to move quickly in the ring was a necessity. He not only wanted to out box the champ, but he also wanted to be faster afoot than Fitzgerald.

Each morning Dean would serve the Mass, and each day he became a regular communicant. Each time that Father Dillon placed the little wafer on Dean's tongue became something special. He always felt different after having Communion. He couldn't quite determine what was happening to him, but it made him feel closer to God. Serving Mass and receiving Communion daily brought Dean closer to his dream, a dream which Dean would one day very soon share with Father Dillon. It made him feel special when he thought about it.

Dean hurried to the gym. Max came out of his office quickly to greet him. His new sparring partner, Luke Harradaway, the lightweight, was already in the ring shadow boxing.

"Hi, Dean. I want you to meet Luke. He's had eight fights and has won all of them. I told Luke about our plans, and he will be available for a week or so. Get your gloves on and join us."

It didn't take long for Dean to get his equipment on and climb into the ring. Max introduced him to Luke. The two touched gloves. Max told Dean and Luke that he would like them to go three or four rounds. That would allow both fighters to get to know each other. Each man went to his corner, and Max rang a bell for the first round. Luke moved lightly about the ring, with Dean moving in close enough to fire a few right labs. Luke instinctively moved away, but never moved straight back. He, too, must have had a careful trainer. Luke's left hand jabs touched Dean's chin and cheeks, but Dean was also bobbing and moving from side to side. He caught Luke with his left jab, and he noticed a smile on Luke's face. Both men traded punches as the round ended.

Each of the rounds went about the same way. Neither fighter suffered any damage. Max called it at the end of the fourth round. The two young fighters headed for the showers.

While dressing, Dean thanked Luke for being one of his sparring partners. The two shook hands. They would see each other the rest of the week.

"Well, son," Max said, "what did you think of Luke?"

"He moves well," said Dean. "He certainly has some neat jabs, and I have a feeling that he may also have some bigger punches, too." Max nodded and went into his office. Dean left for St. Jude.

The first week went by. Dean continued his daily visits with Father Dillon. They stopped at the hospital, and Dean asked the nurse about Stella.

"Oh, didn't you hear? She has gone home. She still has to have her chemo, but she has been feeling a lot better, good enough to want to go home."

Those words made Dean feel very good. Each evening when he said his prayers, he would always remember to ask God to help the sick and the dying. Dean made a special request that God be near and close to Stella. Maybe his prayers were being answered. Dean finished his evening prayers, thanked God for watching over the sick and the dying, especially Stella, and then he climbed into bed. His dream was indeed coming true.

Max was waiting for Dean at the gym the next morning.

"I want you to meet Lance Sartell, another of our sparring partners. He's had ten fights and won them all. As a welterweight, Lance will give you an opportunity to box someone in your weight class."

Max introduced Dean and Lance; the two fighters shook hands. Lance was a heavier puncher than Luke. Unlike Luke, Lance liked to brawl a bit. Dean felt the power in Lance's punches. He also felt what it was like to have someone clinch and punch.

Max was quick to shout, "Keep your mid-section

protected with your elbows. Move! You don't want to be a stationary target for a heavy puncher."

Dean heard Max's remarks. He didn't allow Lance to clinch again. Dean also managed to get in his own shots at Lance's mid-section, and so went each of the afternoon workouts with Lance.

The week ended. Max paid Lance. The two exchanged thanks, and Dean said, "Sure hope you can see my fight against Fitzgerald. If you need some extra tickets, I know Max will be able to get them for you." Lance indicated that he would be cheering for him. Dean thanked Max for bringing in Lance and Luke.

It was just two weeks before the Fitzgerald fight. Dean still had one more sparring partner to help him polish up his boxing skills, and then he'd be ready for the non-title fight. Max had a thirty-one year old journeyman middleweight named Julian Perez as Dean's final sparring partner. Perez had been in many fights against some of the best middleweights in the business. Though he had never had a championship bout, he had been ranked in the top ten. Like Father Dillon, Perez had never realized his dream. He was also a southpaw. Though Fitzgerald was better known for his right hand jabs and punches, he had also fought two of his opponents as a southpaw. Max wasn't going to take any chances. Perez's southpaw style would be yet another of Max's precautions in Dean's preparation.

Again, the two men were introduced; they climbed into the ring, and Max barked out different techniques for Dean to use against Perez. The third day that the two met in Max's ring, Perez caught Dean with a vicious left hand and followed up with a smashing right which almost caught Dean squarely on the chin. Dean back pedaled immediately, and for the first time since he had worked with Max, Dean felt what a knockout punch really felt like. He felt light headed for just a few seconds. Perez moved in, and Dean clinched a sparring partner for the first time. The round ended, but Dean had greater respect for Perez, and he listened carefully to what Max had to say about his encounter with Perez.

"You can't be careless at any time in a fight. If you start drifting or dreaming, you'll pay the price. A champion boxer is always' looking for those weaknesses. Fitz didn't get to be the champ by making costly mistakes. You've got to beat him at his own game. You've got to outsmart, out box, and out punch your opponents. Most importantly, you must always be alert. If and when your opponent makes a mistake, you must make him pay for his mistake." With those words, Max told Dean to hit the showers.

That evening, as usual, Dean said his prayers. Again his prayers included Max and Father Dillon. He thanked God for allowing him to meet two very special people: Max and Father Dillon. He asked his God to give him the strength, the courage, and the ability to win his next two fights. He wasn't too sure that he should be asking God about boxing things, especially with so many people suffering and dying throughout the world, but he also knew that God was an all- caring Person and that his boxing had created some very tangible rewards; it had brought many fallen away parishioners back to St. Jude; it had helped Sluice and his friends to become better people; it had helped an old priest to realize a dream, and last but not least, it had brought Dean closer to his dream.

The local newspaper carried daily articles about the upcoming non-title fight. One article included a picture of Dean with the caption: "Altar boy to test his boxing skills against the champ." Another picture showed Dean receiving Communion. He remembered the camera flashes a few weeks back. Other photos had also been taken since that first shot, but this was the first time that Dean's picture headed the article. Father Dillon had also seen and read the article.

"You're a celebrity from my church. Why, I've had more people receiving Communion in one week than I had all last year. The bishop called and asked whether or not I could use an assistant priest to help with the overflow. Thanks to you, Dean, I'm also becoming a celebrity. Can't say that I dislike it either. I heard more confessions in the past two weeks than I've heard in the last three years. The majority of the confessions are very sincere. Again, thanks to you, Catholics who had fallen away from attending Mass and Communion are coming back. I never thought that this would happen to me, but I am enjoying being a priest ever so much. God must be also pleased."

With those words, Father Dillon walked briskly

into his office. Dean saw the smile on the priest's face, and he also flashed a similar smile.

Only a little over a week remained before Dean would be climbing into the ring with Fitzgerald, the welterweight champion of the world. He knew this final week's workouts would fine tune him for the bout. He would listen carefully to Max's every word. He would concentrate on what he had to do in order to give the champ a good fight, and with some luck, he might just win the fight. He was confident, and he was certainly ready.

Max approached Dean as he entered the gym. "I'm going to have another fighter on the under card of your fight. Sluice will begin his pro career with a four round match. I was wondering if you would go a few rounds with him so he gets the feeling of being in with a real fighter."

Dean hesitated. He remembered the beating he had taken from Sluice and his buddies. He remembered how Sluice had ridiculed Father Dillon at the playground. He remembered his hatred of Sluice when Sluice swore at Father Dillon, but he also remembered his previous professional fights; he remembered Sluice and his buddies watching him win; he remembered how Sluice had thanked him for helping him give up his gang activities. Yes, Dean would spar a few rounds with Sluice, now his friend.

Max had each of the fighters wear boxing headgear. Max remained in Sluice's corner. The bell sounded. The two met in the center of the ring and touched gloves.

Dean threw a few quick jabs at Sluice, who blocked the punches. Unlike Dean, Sluice was a puncher. He found it difficult to box when Max insisted he box, and even though he was now a friend, he had a mean look on his face. Sluice tried to force Dean into a corner. He fired a bolo shot at Dean's head. Dean was moving away, so the punch only grazed his head. Dean kept jabbing with his right and then with his left. Sluice had trouble blocking these quick punches. It was quite obvious that Dean was in better shape and was considerably more skilled than Sluice. Sluice clinched Dean, and at the break he fired two quick punches to Dean's mid-section. Dean was moving, but he did feel the force of these punches; he knew that Sluice, with Max's help, would one day be an up and coming fighter. Max sounded the bell.

With the rounds over, the two fighters left for the showers with arms stretched over one another's shoulders. Both were smiling, and both were thanking each other for the sparring rounds.

Sluice turned to Dean, "I really want to thank you for all that you've done for me and the boys. You've turned our lives around, like serving Mass, and we have nothing but respect for Father Dillon. Father has been helping each of us to make our confessions. Won't be very long, and we'll be receiving daily Communion. Never ever thought this would happen to me, but again thanks." Sluice showered, dressed, and left the gym.

Dean knew now that his God was very much involved in his life. He knew God had turned Sluice and his buddies around. He would remember to thank God when he said his evening prayers.

The day before the fight, Dean went with Father Dillon on his daily tour. They stopped at the orphanage. Dean enjoyed his visits with the children. They loved it when he read stories to them. He had the habit of dramatizing each story. He would watch the children's reactions to his dramatic skills. He loved visiting with them. He vowed to do this more often.

Their next stop was the hospital, and again Dean visited the terminally ill. He gently held their hands and looked softly into their eyes. He wondered what each of the patients was thinking during those special moments. He knew that God loved each of these persons, but again, Dean felt guilty. Why must these people have to suffer so much? Though the question had no specific answer, Dean still thought about it. He tried to understand God's ways. Maybe he would understand someday. After their visits, the two walked slowly back to St. Jude. This would be Dean's final night before the big fight.

Dean changed into his pajamas and knelt by his bed. It was important this evening that his prayers included those people and things which were special in his life. He thought about the day's events. Dean especially wanted his God to understand why Father Dillon and Max were so intensely concerned about Dean's non-title fight. In a sense, both Max and Father were reliving their lives. Each of the men had had special dreams that had really never been realized. It wasn't that boxing and fighting were the only things in one's life, but prize fighting had left a void in each of their lives. Dean's successes were beginning to fill those voids.

Success was also one of Father Dillon's drawbacks. He had been unsuccessful as a boxer; he felt he was somewhat of a failure as a parish priest. With Dean's arrival, all of this was changing. His church was filled with converts and fallen away Catholics. His Sunday sermons were more meaningful.

Max also seemed to have found a new meaning in his life. His gym was being used by some of the promising boxers. His services were being sought by other trainers and managers.

Dean's next thoughts focused on Sluice and his buddies. Thanks to Dean's efforts, all of these young men were turning around their lives. Instead of cursing and hurting others, these young men had become active altar boys at St. Jude.

Before climbing into bed, Dean's final thoughts dwelt on his next fight. If he could have a good showing, he might be in line for a title shot. He might be just two fights away from having Max and Father Dillon realize their dreams. In a soft whisper, he asked God to watch over him. He knew that his request might not be considered to be an important one, but Dean knew that God's presence was deeply needed. He didn't simply want to win the fight for his own reasons; he wanted to win for the two men who had stepped into his life.

God, he knew, would understand Dean's feelings. Dean made the sign of the cross and climbed into bed.

The next morning included Mass, Communion, and another special fighter's breakfast. Mary wanted to do her part to help Dean realize his dream, even though no one really knew what Dean's dream dealt with, but they would all know sooner than later.

Dean visited the gym for the final day. Max was waiting, and he directed Dean into his office. Dean was surprised to see Father Dillon already seated. Dean took a chair and looked carefully at the two men. Max was the first to speak.

"Father and I have been carefully thinking about your next fight. We both share the same feelings, that maybe we are pushing you too fast. We've been thinking that we really haven't sat down to find out what you want in life. We've been selfish in our dealings with you, but we want you to know that if you were to decide that you didn't want this fight, that we would understand and we would be willing to call it off. We could always claim a slight hand injury."

Before Max had finished those words, Dean quickly replied, "I came to Father Dillon's as a homeless wanderer, but you two have brought new meaning to my life. Without Father Dillon's open heart and your fatherly coaching, I could still be looking for a place to sleep and a place to eat. I'm not faced with that type of life anymore, thanks to you gentlemen. Max, you've been like the father I really never had, and Father, you have become my spiritual father. Neither of you has ever forced me to do anything that I didn't want to do. Some how or other, I'm the one who thinks that he has been the intruder. I had been told before coming to St. Jude that Father Dillon would take me in for a few weeks until I was back on my feet. I've stayed beyond that invitation. It's almost as if I've found a permanent home. I know that I will have many decisions to make in determining my future plans, but if you will allow me, I am hoping that you will be involved in helping me plan my future. I love both of you dearly, and I hope that in some ways you feel the same about me. I truly would be lost if I was asked to leave the two of you. As for the fight, I wouldn't train as I have if I didn't like doing what I'm doing, and what I will do. You both are major parts of my life." After those remarks, Dean pressed the shoulders of the two men.

Father Dillon was the first to speak. "You're a great kid and a great person. I knew that when we met months ago. The first time you entered my house, we talked about the fighter that was on T.V. Your comments about the fighter were so precise. I knew right then that I might have someone special visiting with me. As I got to know you better, and after the episode on the playground with Sluice and his buddies, I felt that maybe, with my encouragement, that you might consider a boxing career. I had had another boy who showed similar talents, but it just didn't work out with him. You were so different; you seemed to thrive on being an altar boy, on visiting the sick with me, the homeless, Max's gym, and the other places on my daily tours. When you agreed to begin working out at Max's place, I knew that I had found someone who just might make my special dream come true. I wish to apologize for steering you into a life which you may not want or like." With that the priest turned to Max.

It didn't take Max too long to air his views.

"When I first saw you in my gym's ring, I knew that you were a very special talent. Oh, I had seen others who might also have met the challenge which a boxing career requires, but none of them had the inner heart which you possessed. When you asked me about why I said, 'son', I felt that I wanted to be more than just an ex-pug trainer. I wanted to watch over you like a father would watch over his son, and so our relationship grew. Like Father Dillon's life, you have also brought new meaning to my life, and I wish to thank you for that."

Max extended his open hand, and Dean extended his. Father Dillon put his arm around the two. A bond of friendship had been secured.

"I believe we have a fight to prepare for!" The two men smiled and went about their duties.

Twenty

Fight Night

THE ARENA WAS packed to the rafters. Dean wouldn't have to worry about fans. Thousands were on hand to watch this fight. Max, Father Dillon, and Dean went into the dressing room.

"Before I wrap your hands, I want you to exercise a bit, shadow box a little. I want you a bit sweaty when you put on your sweat shirt and robe. You have to be ready for the fight. There are two prelims before you enter the ring. One of those prelims is Sluice's four rounder. I'll be in Sluice's corner during that first match, I'll be back with you and Father Dillon before the second prelim is over to discuss our final preparations." With those comments, Max left the room.

Sluice was in an adjacent room. Max wrapped Sluice's hands and helped him put on his gloves. One could tell by looking at Sluice's face that he was nervous, but like Dean, he too, was looking forward to his first fight. Max whispered something to his young fighter, and the two left for the ring. The ring announcer introduced Sluice's challenger, Dale Boston, who was fighting out of Flint, Michigan.

Then he turned to Sluice's corner. "In the blue corner, one of our local boxers, Bob 'Sluice' Major, comes into this fight weighing 151 pounds, wearing the white shorts with the black stripe." The announcer also mentioned that this was the first professional fight for both boxers.

Max took the towel from Sluice's neck as the bell for the first round sounded. Dale was the taller of the two, but Sluice was the more muscular. Dale's quick jabs were nicely blocked by Sluice, who appeared to be confident and ready for his first fight. Sluice feinted a left and pounded his right into Dale's protected face. He was fighting aggressively. He plunged forward with both hands firing away. His right was blocked, but his left hand scored heavily, and Dale was forced to clinch. Rounds two and three were much the same, Dale throwing jabs, and Sluice throwing the harder punches.

Max wiped the sweat from Sluice's face. "You've got him beat," said Max, "but you have to keep throwing punches to win."

By round four it was still a close match. "Protect your chin and your mid-section. When you throw punches, you need to move your head and your feet faster, and remember not to go straight back. He is a light puncher, but you don't want him to land a lucky punch."

With those final words, Sluice answered the bell for round four. Again Sluice threw the heavier punches, but Dale threw more jabs. The fight was either fighter's to win.

After the final bell, the announcer indicated that it was a split decision with the decision favoring Sluice. A huge smile crossed Sluice's face when the ref raised his arm in victory. He put his hands up over his head and accepted the applause from the audience.

As the two left the ring, Max whispered to Sluice, "It's important to win your first fight." They went on to the dressing room.

Dean was still shadow boxing when Max entered the room. "Well, we won the first fight of the evening. It wasn't the best opener that I've ever seen, but Sluice listened carefully and followed all of my instructions. I think, with a lot of hard work, that Bob 'Sluice' Major could have an interesting career. He's a rough diamond now, but he'll improve with each of his fights." Then Max began wrapping Dean's outstretched hands.

Father Dillon and Max would both be in Dean's corner for this fight. Max would act as trainer and cut man. The three walked slowly to the ring apron. The fans roared their approval for this gladiator, this altar boy, this local fighter.

Dean sat quietly on his stool as the announcer said, "In the blue corner, wearing black trunks with white stripes, the challenger, a local fighter, weighing in at 148 pounds, altar boy Dean Nelson."

The crowd's noise forced the announcer to wait a few moments before introducing Bob Fitzgerald. "Fighting out of Lansing, Michigan, weighing 149 pounds, the welterweight champion of the world, Bob Fitzgerald!"

Fitzgerald raised his hand and received a loud audience response. Both fighters were quite popular, and both had many fans sitting in the arena. While sitting on his stool, Dean looked out at those who had ringside seats. Just rows away were Doc, Mary, Sluice and his buddies, and Luke, Lance, and Julian, his sparring partners. Last, but not least, Dean saw Stella sitting near the end of the row with a neatly dressed gentleman. She no longer wore a scarf to cover her hair. A huge smile crossed her beautiful face, and Dean also smiled and lifted one of his gloves. She and her male friend noticed Dean's slight gesture. The two were holding hands. As Dean observed them, he realized that his God was present in the huge arena. He knew this after seeing Stella's face and the face of her friend. Was it possible? Had Stella's cancer been controlled? Had it gone into remission? If either had happened, Dean's nightly prayers had indeed been answered. Without thinking of where he was, Dean made the sign of the cross and whispered, "Thank you, Lord." Dean was more than ready for Fitzgerald; he had someone very special in his corner.

The ref beckoned the two fighters to the center of

the ring and gave them their final instructions. They touched gloves and went to their corners.

Max was the first to speak. "Remember everything that I told ya. You got to jab and move, jab and move. Avoid getting caught in the corners or on the ropes. Stay in the middle of the ring; protect your chin and your mid-section, and give him plenty of head and leg movement."

The bell sounded for round one. Both men went again to the center of the ring and touched gloves. Dean respected Fitzgerald. After all, he was the champ. It wasn't long before both fighters were firing their jabs. Not much damage was done by either fighter as the feeling out procedure continued into the second and third rounds. Round four found both fighters picking up the pace. Dean realized that his daily running and sprinting were paying off. When he sat on his stool at the end of the fourth round, he was hardly tired. In fact, he felt stronger than in any previous fight.

Round five started out fast. Fitzgerald was moving in closer to Dean. He fired a few jabs at Dean's face and head, and then he went downstairs with combinations to Dean's body. Though Dean was able to ward off most of the punches, they were heavier and more precisely targeted. As the bell sounded, Dean felt that he might lose this round.

"Remember what I told you when we watched the champ's fight against Batch? The champ may start as early as the sixth round trying to slow you down. Meet punches with punches, and move!"

With these instructions, Dean was ready for the sixth round. The champ didn't waste any time. He immediately tried to force Dean into a corner. He fired punches into Dean's mid-section. Dean was ready for the onslaught and inflicted some of his own punishment. He caught the champ with a hard right and left to the mid-section, and he scored with another hard right and left to the champ's partially protected chin. These punches brought cheers from the lively crowd. Round six ended.

Max put a piece of cold metal on a swollen area directly under Dean's right eye.

"Nothing to worry about," Max said. "Keep up the good work; you've got him thinking."

Rounds seven and eight were evenly scored for both fighters, but good old Max had noticed something special. "Listen carefully, Dean. The champ is beginning to slow a bit. He is also beginning to lean forward, especially when you go to his mid-section. I think you might catch him with your straight right hand, and if you do, you might put him down for the count. This fight is very close. A knockdown might bring the fight our way, but you have to be very careful. You can't give away your strategy."

Dean listened carefully to what Max was saying. He had never had a killer's instinct, but he also wanted to help two very dear friends realize their dreams. The bell sounded for round nine.

Fitzgerald came out very fast. He tried to catch Dean by surprise, but Dean was ready for his charge.

He fired out three quick jabs and then followed with his left. Fitzgerald caught the force of the blows with his gloves, but he continued to get in close and to fire away at Dean's body. With only a few seconds left in the round, Dean noticed that Fitzgerald went straight back, and Dean saw what Max was talking about. Dean fired a short left to the body and a straight right to that open spot. His right hand caught the champ on the side of his cheek and ear. He tried to compose himself, but the force of Dean's blows forced him to go down on one knee. The ref motioned for Dean to go to a neutral corner while he began to count. Fitz got up at the count of six, and the ref brushed off the champ's gloves. As Dean moved in, the round ended.

"I knew you could do it!" uttered Father Dillon. "You really got his attention with that right hand!"

Max also had some special comments for Dean. "The champ is getting tired. He's beginning to lean forward when he gets in close. When he does that, fire an uppercut with either hand. You might catch him squarely on the chin. If nothing else, it will help us to win round ten. I don't want you to forget all that we have worked for this past few weeks. Whatever you do, don't get careless. A hurt fighter can be a dangerous fighter." As Max spoke those final words, the bell rang for round ten.

It was just the way Max had said. Fitzgerald knew that it was a close fight; he knew that the knockdown in round nine could have been the fatal blow. He was not about to make the same mistake. He still bore in on Dean, hoping to score his own knockdown, but Dean sensed that the champ's blows were no longer as forceful as they were in the early rounds. Dean waited like a fox with its prey. The champ fired two quick punches to Dean's mid-section, and as he did, he leaned slightly forward. Dean quickly fired a right uppercut which caught the champ squarely on the chin. Hurt again, the champ tried to clinch, but Dean fired his left and the champ went reeling backwards. He didn't go down, but he was hurt. Dean saw the frustration on Fitzgerald's face, but he wasn't going to do anything foolish. He went back to his jabs as the round and the fight ended.

"You did it, son; I've never seen a better tactical fight. You're a true listener. If my boxing experience means anything, I think we just won a close decision over the welterweight champion of the world." Max smiled and wiped the sweat from Dean's face, neck, and head.

Father Dillon was the next to speak. "I can't believe that you've come this far in such a short time! You were in complete control of this fight! I just can't imagine you losing this one!"

The ring announcer took the mike. "We have a unanimous decision. Judge Abrams has the fight 95 to 91. Judge Rius scored it 95 to 93, and Judge Ridgeway has the fight 95 to 90 in favor of the St. Jude's altar boy, Dean Nelson."

Dean could not believe the announcement, but he knew it was true when Max and Father Dillon each put their arms around his neck. There were tears in the priest's eyes. His life long dream was being realized.

Max also embraced his young fighter. "I said that I wouldn't let anyone hurt my son." Unashamedly, he wiped away the collecting moisture from his eyes. Dean stood up and immediately went over to the champ's corner. The champ put his arm around Dean's neck, and the two men walked around the ring to the deafening roar of the crowd. Everyone was on his feet.

Another ring announcer cornered Dean and asked him what his plans were. Would he seek a title shot? Dean didn't feel it was something he should answer. He politely referred the announcer to his trainer, Max, and to his manager, Father Dillon. These two had made all of the decisions for his previous fights. There was no reason now for Dean to be making those decisions. Max, Father, and Dean left the ring and went back to their dressing room. Dean caught the eye of Stella and her friend. He noticed her lips moving, uttering thanks. He raised one of his gloves so she knew he had seen and heard her. Winning the fight was one thing, but Stella's smiling face beamed even greater. Dean realized that God was present and performing miracles, Stella's health being one of them. For the first time in his young life, Dean had found the true meaning of friendship and love. He knew that his final dream would insure extended love to all of his closest friends.

Twenty-one

A Great Opportunity

Several weeks went by. Dean continued his tour each day with Father Dillon. He could hardly go anywhere without a reporter there to ask questions. The same old questions were asked each time. Do you have any immediate plans to fight the champ again? Are your managers lining up any future fights? How long do you plan to stay at St. Jude? Dean just wasn't the person to be answering these questions. He usually told them to contact Father Dillon or Max or both, and that was the end of the questioning.

Dean got up rather early one morning. He went to the porch, and the daily newspaper had already arrived. He opened it to the sport section. The headlines immediately caught his eye. "Randy Batch Injures His Right Hand." The article continued, "Batch's return match will have to be cancelled or changed to a much later date." Dean didn't know what to say or think. He

A Great Opportunity

did ask himself one very important question. Would Max and Father be getting a call from Fitzgerald's manager? He hurried into the kitchen where Father was seated.

"I see you've read the morning news. I heard about it on the radio last evening. Seems that Batch hit one of his sparring partners with a heavy right hand and injured it in the process. X-rays were taken immediately, and a small break in the wrist area was noticed. It appears that his return fight with Fitzgerald has been cancelled indefinitely. Since Fitzgerald had been training for this fight, the champ might consider fighting another fighter. Your name came up, but neither I nor Max has received any call about that," said Father Dillon.

Dean would have a chance to find out more about this possible fight when he went to Max's gym that afternoon. He finished his chores for Mary, showered, and made his way to Max's gym. Max was on the phone when Dean arrived, and he motioned him to come into his office and take a seat. Dean's pulse was now beating rapidly. Would Max be telling him about the final piece to the puzzle? In a few minutes Dean would hear what Max had to say.

Max put the phone down and looked squarely at Dean. "How would you like a championship fight in eight weeks? I just got off the phone with Fitzgerald's manager. He feels that they owe us a shot at the champ. They also feel that your recent fight with the champ warranted a. return match. He was certain that a match for the title would fill the arena. I didn't give him a yes or no answer, because I wanted to talk with you and also discuss this with Father Dillon. Well, son, do you want to fight for the championship?"

Dean didn't even have to think about such a decision. He knew that this would be the last piece to the puzzle. He wanted to be able to fulfill Father's dream, but he also knew that the next eight weeks could be the hardest he might ever have in his young career.

Dean smiled at Max. "If you think we have a chance to win the fight, I'm all for it," he replied.

"Well, son, I've told you before that I would never put you into the ring to lose. With your talents and your willingness to train, Fitz better be well prepared for this match," uttered Max. "We have our work cut out for us, Dean. We'll have to work on your combinations, your jabs, and your right cross. You'll also have to know how to slip punches or block others. Fitz will study the film of your previous fight. He'll come better prepared for a championship fight than he was for our last encounter. I want your hands always wrapped before sparring or hitting the heavy or light bag. Each day I want you to include some shadow boxing. I want daily use of the medicine ball, with no less than ten drops on your stomach daily. Also, you want to make an effort to breathe through the nose during all sparring sessions. I want 3 minute sessions on the heavy and light bags with a one minute rest in between; we'll use the 16 ounce sparring gloves. We'll use the classic stance with your left foot flat, forward and slightly turned in;

heel of the right foot off the floor; upper body turned slightly left; right hand high and close to the chin; your left just below eye level."

Dean listened carefully to Max's instructions. He had heard these same comments many times. He also knew that he had to fire a number of punches when he chose to go toward his opponent. One punch was never sufficient. He also knew that he had to move his head as well as his feet. He would avoid the cardinal sin of going straight back after throwing his punches, so Fitz couldn't counter punch him.

Max was a perfectionist. Dean knew that he would have to listen carefully to Max's instructions at the end of each round. He also knew that his speed and his overall conditioning would eventually determine the final outcome.

As Dean was preparing to leave the gym, Max commented, "Don't forget your road and speed workouts. The fighter with the most endurance will still be standing when this fight is over."

With those words ringing in his ears, Dean left the gym. The dream which he would be a part of was about to be realized. Father Dillon, Max, and Dean were about to embark on a dream which would affect each of their lives. Dean smiled and headed back to St. Jude.

When Dean got home, Mary was preparing the supper meal, so he sat down. Shortly after, Father joined him. Dean saw the smile on the priest's face. He knew immediately that Max had talked with Father.

Dean asked quickly, "Well, Father, what do you think of Max getting another fight with Fitzgerald? He told me all about it when I went to the gym today. I think you know that I trust Max as I would my father. If he thinks that I have a chance against the champ, I have to believe his confidence in me.

"I don't like to include God in this fight," Dean continued, "but He has answered my prayers, and I plan to thank Him when I say my evening prayers. Did Max tell you the fight is only eight weeks away? That means much of my time will be spent at the gym with Max. I'll still serve the morning Mass, and I want to go with you when you make your daily rounds. I may have to miss a few days, but I can't wait to see some of my friends and tell them about this championship fight. I know they'll all be happy for the three of us.

"After the fight, Father, I'd like to have another conference confession. It's not that I've done anything wrong, but I have a very special reason for having this confession." With those final comments, Dean pushed away from the table and headed for his room.

Father Dillon called after him, "Thank you, Dean, for bringing new meaning into my life!" Then he continued silently, "Your serving Mass each day; your visits with me to those who are sometimes lonely and for those that are sick and dying; your many conversations with me; and finally, your dedication to prize fighting. All of these have inspired me to be a better priest and a better person. My life will never be the same. You are embarking on what Robert Frost would call the 'miles to go before I sleep...' I have lived a good and meaningful life, but until you came into my life, I always felt a sense of guilt.

"Oh, I visited the sick, and I tried to comfort the poor, but I did some of these things sometimes without knowing why. You have changed all of that. When I say the Mass each day, and when I see how reverently you perform as my altar boy, I realize now why I chose to be a priest. True, I had had another dream, but I realize now that being a priest will be the most important part of my remaining life.

"Your coming to St. Jude played a major part in rejuvenating my life, and now your match with the champ will put to rest an important aspect of my life. I don't know how to thank you, Dean, for all that you have done for me. I was just putting in my time, but now I realize that my life has not been a failure, and it took a young man to direct and to show me the light.

Father contemplated those final words as he walked to his room. He hadn't realized that his advice had opened up a new world for Dean.

Dean's final confession with the old priest would chart completely new territory. He wouldn't have to worry about hurting Father's feelings, and if he won his fight with Fitzgerald, their friendship would be forever sealed. Dean said his prayers and then slept soundly through the night.

Dean was up early the next morning. He dressed and walked to the church. He wanted to say a few special prayers before serving the morning Mass. He made the sign of the cross as he knelt in the pew. Each of his prayers was followed by a few special comments. His first Hail Mary was for all of the sick and dying which he visited daily. His second prayer was for all of his friends: Sluice and his buddies, Stella, Mary, Dr. Browman, Jeb Stuart, Addie, and all of his sparring friends. He prayed that none of his friends would realize sickness and or death. His final prayers were for the two people who had influenced his life and his religious faith the most, Max and Father Dillon. Dean pondered his thoughts of Max. Here was a friend and a father figure who had first of all befriended him and who had considered him his son. Dean's prayer for Max was special. He loved this man as though he were his own father. He respected Max's ability to be involved with his development as a prize fighter. After saying his prayer for Max, Dean whispered softly, "Thank you, Max, for your wisdom and for your love."

Last but not least were the special prayers for his closest and dearest friend, Father Dillon. Dean could not begin to thank the priest. He bowed his head and recited the Act of Contrition and the Act of Faith, and he asked God to look over and to protect his aging priest. Again he whispered, "You have given me a new look on life which I shall never forget. Your guidance and your love have helped me to realize my dream." Dean made the sign of the cross again and bowed his head humbly for a few moments.

In a few weeks, Dean would be climbing into the ring with the welterweight champion of the world.

Each day before morning Mass, Dean would run out to the porch to find the morning newspaper. He would turn to the sport pages and read about the title fight. Some of the reporters were picking him to win the fight in a close decision. Dean had never gone more than ten rounds in any of his early or recent fights, and he wondered if he would have the stamina to go the distance. He would have to discuss this with Max.

Each morning, Dean would serve Mass for Father Dillon, eat the breakfast Mary had prepared, make his daily visits to the hospital, the Y, and the homeless shelters, and end up at Max's gym.

One morning when he arrived, Max waved him into his office. "Me and Father Dillon have closed the deal with the Fitzgerald management. Your purse will be one hundred and fifty thousand, and they agreed to a return bout whether we win or lose the fight. We shook hands on it. The paperwork will be ready to sign tomorrow. What do you think of the offer?"

Dean stuttered, "One hundred and fifty thousand for a fight?" That was more money than he might make in his entire lifetime. "It's just great, Max. Thank you, thank you very much." Dean was able to gather himself together saying, "Do you think I can go fifteen rounds and still be standing?"

Max's reply was instantaneous. "You can do whatever you have to do! Don't doubt your abilities, son; I'll have you ready for that fight." Dean left Max's office, got ready for his workout, and climbed into the ring.

Twenty-two

The Preparation

MAX DIDN'T HAVE to bring in any extra sparring partners. With all of the publicity Dean, Father Dillon, and Max had received in recent weeks, Max's gym was always filled with new promising boxers. Even some of the successful fighters frequented the gym.

"Do you have any special instructions for the Fitzgerald fight?" asked Dean.

"I've got three films that I want us to go over when you come the next time. I have the Batch-Fitzgerald bout, our fight, and one other Fitzgerald fight. He fights as a southpaw in one of his other fights. I think it's a good idea to study his southpaw style in that fight also."

Max went about his chores, and Dean showered, dressed, and started walking toward St. Jude. His head was bursting with pictures concerning his fight with the champ and about his own dreams. He hadn't told anyone, but he would soon need to make his most important confession. He could wait for the outcome of the Fitzgerald fight; then he would have that crucial meeting with Father Dillon. Would Father understand? Would the old priest feel that he had been betrayed by him? These questions bothered Dean, but he knew that he could no longer delay this confession.

Articles about the Fitzgerald-Nelson bout appeared in all the newspapers. It was continuously mentioned on the radio. Each day after morning Mass, hundreds of people would wait to see Dean or to get his autograph. He could hardly move so many people crowded around him. "Are you going to knock him out?" yelled one member of the crowd. Dean wasn't about to answer any questions. He had talents, but so did Fitzgerald. He wasn't about to give up any of his thoughts. They might be misinterpreted by members of the press who were mingled among the crowd. Father Dillon was also mobbed, and like Dean, all he would say is, "Come to the fight and see what happens."

After eating breakfast, Dean skipped his daily tour and went immediately to the gym. Max was waiting for him.

"We better go over these films I have for you. I need to point out a number of crucial elements in each of those fights." Max started by showing Dean the fight with Fitzgerald as a southpaw. "Watch closely how Fitz's opponent moves. He never allows Fitz to hit him with his big left punch. He also stays out of the corners. Much of the fight is fought in the middle of the ring, but again, like our fight, Fitz points to the sixth, seventh, and eighth rounds to do his heavier fighting. He constantly focuses on his opponent's mid-section. He's almost religious about that, but I also noticed that his own protection of his chin, chest, and face are exposed to punches. His opponent wasn't fast enough to capitalize on these openings, but we'll certainly be ready for them."

The second fight was the Batch fight. "There is no doubt in my mind that Fitz knew about Batch's punching power. You'll notice in the first four rounds, and possibly the fifth, that Fitz uses his speed and footwork to outmaneuver his slower opponent. Again, we'll up our speed and outbox Fitz in those early rounds. If we're going to win by a decision, we'll need to win some of the early rounds."

Max switched to the Dean-Fitz fight. Dean didn't have to hear very much from Max about this fight, but Max emphasized what he had so often said to him. "Everything you do right will come off of your jabs, and your head and foot movement. Most importantly, never go straight back when you are using your jabs. If you remember what you have seen on these films and what I have pointed out to you, you should have no problems with Fitz. Concentration will be your greatest attribute. Remember that. I'll also leave the projector and the films in my office. You may want to study them further. Your senses are so sharp that you might see some other weaknesses which I failed to point out to you."

The Preparation

Max hit Dean on the seat of his shorts and told him to hit the showers. Dean did so and hurried home.

Mary and Father Dillon were setting the table when Dean came in. Immediately the priest said, "I understand that Max has been reviewing three of Fitz's fights. After having seen Fitz in those fights, what are your estimates of his abilities?"

Dean responded quickly. "First of all, Fitz is in superb condition. His boxing techniques are very good. He doesn't make too many mistakes, and he covers up carefully if and when he does make a mistake. We did notice one thing which Fitz did in our fight and also in his other two fights. He boxes for at least five rounds, mostly jabbing. Jabs and a lot of foot and head movements are accentuated in the early rounds, but in rounds six, seven, and eight, he moves in closer to his opponent and seems to concentrate on the midsection. Fitz knows that I'm familiar with this form of attack, since he also used it against me. He may change his tactics and go earlier or to the later rounds. I'll have to watch his moves carefully and meet his punches with my own. I know one thing, though. He'll be a lot tougher this time than in our last fight."

After those remarks, Dean sat down at the table, made the sign of the cross, and uttered a before meal prayer. Father Dillon smiled, and he, too, bowed his head and prayed.

Though it was not overly late, Dean retired to his room. He still had some of Father's books to read. He noted his book marker and was soon involved in his book. He pushed back his chair a bit, closed his book, and for a few moments he pondered life since coming to St. Jude. He had befriended an old priest; he had met an aged fighter; and in just a few days, he would be fighting the welterweight champion of the world. Was this reality? Was this supposed to happen this way? Was his God directing him to pursue this road? Was he simply feeling sorry for Father Dillon and Max? He thought, "If God is the center of all that is living, then these happenings are not mere chance. What is about to happen to me will serve a definite purpose."

Dean thought long and hard about his last statement. If God was his motivation, then it was natural that God would be watching over Father Dillon, Max, and himself, because their lives would be affected by his actions. He thought about this final conclusion. He liked the fact that his God would be close, and that mattered. Dean slipped to his knees, made the sign of the cross, and whispered, "Thank you, dear Lord, for directing me to Father Dillon's parish; thank you for allowing me to meet so many wonderful people, and though I have not revealed my dream to Father or to Max, these two have played a most important part in my life."

FATHER USED TO complain because he hadn't been able to convert new parishioners, but even his six o'clock Mass was filled each morning. Dean felt that he also had converted some fallen away souls such as Stella,

Addie, and especially, Sluice and his buddies. He felt good about those accomplishments. In a sense, Dean was also instrumental in turning Max and Father Dillon's lives around. The coming championship bout would be his next adventure. It had to be successful. Dean climbed slowly into his bed. It wasn't very long before a dream seemed to relive his life at St. Jude.

When he awakened the next morning, he showered, dressed, and walked briskly to the church chapel. Father Dillon was already putting on his garments.

"Sleep good?" asked the priest.

"You bet!" was Dean's reply, "but I did have a lot of dreams, including one about the fight. But it was a good dream."

After the morning Mass, on their way from the chapel, Dean hurriedly mentioned that after his next fight, he wanted to have a conference confession.

Father looked rather strangely at Dean. "I've never heard of a conference confession, but I'm certain you'll explain it to me when we meet for that special confession."

"You can count on that!" Dean replied. He smiled broadly as he left for Max's gym.

After Dean had completed his final preparation for the Fitzgerald fight, Max studied him carefully. "Well, son, I've done all I can to get you ready for this fight. I don't think this will be your last opportunity to fight a championship bout, but you're getting the chance which Father and me never had. Win or lose, it'll be something very special in your young life. You'll be able to say that you fought the welterweight champion of the world, and not too many other young fighters will be able to say that. If you win, you'll be the dream for many up and coming fighters, including Sluice, and maybe some of his buddies. You'll have thousands of fans who will just want to see you or have you sign an autograph. Think about it, son, one fight, one win catapults you to fame, and should you win, my fortunes will also be realized. Because of the fights which you have won, my gym is nearly full every single day. Thanks to you, I was able to fix up the place, and I've had calls from many managers who want me to train their fighters. Win or lose, you have put new life into my life, and I will never be able to repay you."

"Max," Dean replied, "you have spent hours working with me. Without your skills, I wouldn't be the contender that I am. Thank you for being my trainer and my father figure. Your love and your kindness have spurred me on in my development. I only hope that I won't let Father and you down." With these finals words, Dean headed for the showers.

Twenty-three

The Championship Bout

The next morning, Dean followed Father to the sacristy where they both put on their garments for the early morning Mass. This was a very special day for Dean, the day that he would be fighting for the welterweight championship of the world; the day when he would be able to help Father Dillon realize his life's dream; and the day he would have his conference confession later in the evening. How would Father Dillon respond to his confession? Would he understand? Would he accept Dean's comments about his life, about his future fighting plans? This was indeed a special Mass, and Dean's prayers were said directly to his God.

"Please, dear Lord, allow me to win this fight for Max and for Father Dillon. I know that winning a fight may not be one of the more important things to pray for, but it will allow me to repay Father and Max for what they have done for me."

Dean recited the Hail Mary and the Our Father prayers and finished his requests with the sign of the cross. He bowed his head when Father gave him his Communion. Again, something he could not explain seemed to engulf him.

After the Mass was over, the two removed their garments and headed for one of Mary's famous breakfasts. Dean had to be at Max's gym by 5:00 p.m., and Max would drive them to the arena for his 8:00 p.m. battle.

They arrived at the arena at 6:00 p.m. Max was not one to say much prior to a fight. He felt that he had already conveyed to Dean the strategy for the fight. He wrapped Dean's hands and had him shadow box so that he could build up a slight sweat before entering the ring. He didn't want Dean entering the ring cooled.

It wasn't long before Father came into their locker room. He pressed Dean's shoulder.

"I'm confident you can do it, Dean. I know that Max is supremely confident, too. He told me that if anyone was ready and prepared, that you are. Remember, win or lose, we are very proud of you. You probably don't realize it, but your efforts have gone a long way to make me a better person and a better priest, and for those reasons I can only say thank you for altering my life. Oh, by the way, you have also helped me to realize a dream which I have had for the better part of my life."

Father didn't elaborate on this dream, but Dean knew what the priest's dream was, and he was about to help both Max and Father to realize their dreams.

The arena was packed to the rafters. Dean's closest friends had ringside seats. He anxiously searched their faces as he climbed into the ring.

The ring announcer solemnly introduced the fighters. "In the white corner, wearing white trunks with the black stripe, weighing in at 146 pounds, the heralded altar boy from St. Jude, the challenger Dean Nelson.

"In the red corner, wearing red trunks with the white stripe, the welterweight champion of the world, Bob Fitzgerald, also weighing in at 146 pounds." The referee went to the center of the ring and motioned for the two fighters to touch gloves and fight a clean fight.

Dean went back to his corner and took a quick glance at his friends in the ringside seats. He made the sign of the cross as the bell sounded for round one.

Both fighters moved swiftly to the center of the ring. Fitz was the first to throw his jab, but Dean was moving away, and the jab failed to hit its target. Dean fired two right jabs and then moved away. Fitz followed, but his jabs were light and ineffective. This feeling-out process continued until the bell ended the round.

"He's using the same strategy as he used in the Batch fight. He's going to jab and hit for at least four or five rounds, and then I expect him to go to your midsection," uttered Max. "I want you to speed up your jabs, look for a chance to use your uppercut right, and hit him with your left if and when you get that opportunity. I want him to think that we have changed our fight plans for this bout."

The bell sounded for round two. Though both fighters were feeling each other out, Dean was able to force Fitz into a corner, and Dean fired two straight punches to Fitz's mid-section. When he backed away, he saw a strange look on Fitz's face. Dean's two punches had gotten Fitz's attention. Dean was able to follow up with a series of right and left jabs. The bell ended round two.

"Great, son!" were Max's opening words. "You have him guessing. I want you to do the same in rounds three, four, and five."

The bell sounded for round three. Fitz came out much faster in this round, and he came at Dean with multiple jabs. They were much sharper than those in the first two rounds, indicating that Fitz wanted to establish that he was in control of the fight. Dean would change all of that. He hadn't run mile after mile each day and sprinted dozens of times just to allow Fitz to dominate the fight. Dean moved in on Fitz and scored with several jabs. Again he was able to get Fitz pinned in a corner where he opened up straight shots to Fitz's mid-section. He could hear the noise in the arena, and he knew many of the fans were rooting for him.

Round three was Dean's best round in the fight so far. He had established his punching power. Fitz would have to respect these punches. Dean's jab was finding its mark, and Fitz's face was beginning to redden. There was some slight reddening under both of Fitz's eyes. Dean continued to jab at those areas.

The bell sounded for round four. Fitz came out fast and peppered Dean's face, but many of his jabs simply bounced off Dean's gloves. Fitz continued to move in closer. He caught Dean with a straight right to the nose. Dean felt the power of that blow, but he danced away from any further damage.

Round four was clearly Fitz's best round, and Max made that clear when he muttered, "You aren't moving fast enough to avoid those punches. You simply can't stay in front of him when he punches that fast. Hit and move. How many times have I told you that?"

Dean had never heard Max talk that way. Had Max detected something in Fitz's attack? The bell sounded for round five, and Fitz came out fast again. Dean had to move quicker to regain a bit of his confidence. When Fitz stopped his jabbing, Dean opened up with his own barrage of jabs. These caught Fitz by surprise, and he backed away, but Dean followed with a straight right and left. Both were telling blows and Fitz eyed Dean differently. Dean had regained much of his confidence as the round ended.

Max and Father both were quick to mention the upcoming sixth round. Rounds six, seven, and eight would see the champ concentrate his punches on Dean's mid-section, and the results of his barrage would determine how the fight would unfold.

Dean had listened carefully to what Max and Father had said between rounds, and he was ready for

Fitz's body attack. Fitz tried to force Dean into a corner, but Dean wasn't about to let that happen. Fitz fired a number of jabs hoping that Dean would pull his elbows and gloves up to protect his chin, but Dean failed to make that move, and there was a strange look on Fitz's face. Dean noticed this immediately and threw his own jabs at Fitz's swollen face, and then it happened. Almost without realizing it, the champ left his mid-section unprotected, and Dean fired a straight right and left into that area. Dean had hurt Fitz with those punches, and he moved in closer and fired an uppercut that caught the champ's chin. The champ literally charged Dean and was able to clinch the challenger as the bell sounded. Dean hurried to his corner, sat down and listened carefully to Max's comments.

"You did it, son. You hurt him in those exchanges; he'll have to alter his plans. Your uppercut was a beauty, and Fitz made no answer to that punch. I have a feeling that he'll try a similar tactic in this seventh round. You'll have to be ready for some power shots to your mid-section. Fitz knows that will be the only way he can slow you down. Here, take a little water." Max handed Dean a plastic battle.

The bell sounded for round seven, and Max's words turned out to be true. Fitz moved in close so he could fire some of his straight punches, but Dean was again ready for Fitz's attack. Dean danced away to the middle of the ring with the champ in hot pursuit, but Dean stopped short and fired both his left and right at the on coming Fitz. Both punches scored, and Fitz was hurt. Dean moved in, avoided a clinch, and again fired both of his punches at the startled champ. Dean was close enough to see Fitz's eyes as the champ went down to one knee. The champ shook his head, trying to clear his head, and he glared at Dean. The ref began to count, but the bell sounded.

Dean went to his corner and immediately sat down. Father Dillon was the first to speak. "You would have had a knockout had the round not ended. Your punches were devastating. I don't think the champ can weather another round like that."

Max was also quick to note, "He's hurt and he's confused, but don't get foolish now. He still has enough punching power to hurt you. Be smart, son. Box him. Always protect yourself, and keep moving. He's too tired to follow you, so you might catch him again. Unless I miss my guess, you can knock him out in one of the next two rounds."

Round eight saw Fitz stalking Dean as if the challenger was an animal. He was getting desperate; he had to confront the challenger and force him to fight the champ's fight. Dean was not about to let that happen. He sensed that the champ was confused, but Dean wasn't about to play the champ's game. Dean jabbed and moved, jabbed and moved. Dean could tell that the champ was tiring. He moved cautiously toward the champ, fully expecting some counter punches from Fitz, but this didn't happen so Dean fired a straight right followed by a straight left at the almost motionless target directly in front of him. The straight left caught the champ flush in the face. He literally collapsed in the middle of the ring. Fitz tried gamely to get to one knee, but the ref, realizing the champ's condition, signaled that the fight was over. Dean had won the welterweight championship of the world. Max and Father Dillon were waving their towels and jumping up and down.

"You won, son!" shouted Max. "You're the champion of the whole world!"

Father Dillon was even more boisterous as he jumped up and down shouting, "You made my dream come true! I just knew the good Lord would hear my prayers!" He calmed down just long enough to make a hurried sign of the cross.

Dean smiled, but deep down inside he kept thinking about his final confession. Would the old priest understand his reasons, his choices? Those things were still ahead of him, but this was another night, another occasion, another man's dream. He would enjoy the moment even though it would not be the road he would travel, and yes, enjoy. Dean had his dream to pursue with or without Father Dillon's blessings. He had already stayed too long at the priest's home. It was time to move on, but Dean would never forget his friends, and especially Father Dillon and his father-like friend Max. Those two would always play major roles in his future life. Max, the father whom Dean was blessed to meet, and Father Dillon, his spiritual father. What more could a young man hope to find? Father Dillon had been his emotional and religious teacher, and Max had been his trainer and his fatherly figure. Both had taught him about love, sacrifice, physical preparedness, humility, understanding, and tolerance. Father Dillon had introduced him to worship and to God. He had never felt as confident as he did now. He understood more about the good or bad in life and the good or bad in people. He would take the road least traveled by others, but his road would allow him to help those who needed him most.

The deafening noise of the cheering crowd brought Dean back to the ring. The ring announcer was about to announce the decision.

"We have a new welterweight champion of the world, Dean Nelson!" The crowd was already standing and cheering. In the front row of the arena were Dean's closest friends. Dean waved to them and saw Sluice waving and smiling. In some ways Sluice was one of his closest friends. This was what life was all about. Though it included anger and yes, hate, these emotions could be resolved. Dean remembered his encounter with Sluice and his buddies, but because of him, Sluice and his buddies were in the process of changing and bettering their lives. Dean climbed out of the ring with his trainer Max and his manager Father Dillon. They exited the arena.

Max took off Dean's gloves and then the wraps on his hands. "Well, son, how do you feel? You know, Fitzgerald may want a rematch with you," Max uttered.

"I'll have to wait and see," was all Dean had to say.

"I want to enjoy our victory a while before I consider going back into the ring again. You'll have Sluice to work with and, after this fight you'll probably have other fighters to train."

Dean showered and dressed to return to St. Jude. He had plenty to think about, but he would have other days to do that.

Twenty-four

Future Plans

THE NEXT MORNING, Dean was up early. He had gotten the morning paper and was reading the sport page. Huge letters ran across the top of the page:

> ALTAR BOY NELSON DEFEATS FITZGERALD FOR THE WELTERWEIGHT CHAMPIONSHIP OF THE WORLD.

The sport section had a huge picture of Dean standing in the ring, looking down at the fallen champion. Dean liked the story which followed, but he realized that in another sense this was what life was all about, success and failure. He had wished no harm on Fitzgerald, but now Fitz's life would obviously change. He would no longer be the world champ. He would have to redirect his life and hope to be more successful, or forget what had just happened and go on with his life in the ring. All of us are faced daily with numerous decisions, some good and some bad. That's what life really is all about. Dean also had a huge decision to share with Father Dillon and Max. What would be the outcome?

As he prepared for the morning Mass, Dean knew that it was time for him to have that special confession. He had given much thought to what he would say and do.

Father Dillon came into the little sacristy to put on his garments. "I suppose you've already read the sport section of the newspaper. You are the celebrity of our neighborhood. Why, they are already talking about the rematch with Fitzgerald. I'll bet you can hardly wait for the return match!"

Dean heard Father's comments, but he chose to disregard them. Instead he said, "I'd like to have you hear my confession after Mass today. It can't wait!"

The priest looked carefully at Dean. "If what you're asking is true, I'll be more than willing to hear your confession."

After the Mass concluded, Dean and Father Dillon put away their garments and went directly to the confessional. Dean opened the door and stepped in. He knelt on the padded kneeler. The little curtained door opened slowly.

"In the name of the Father, and of the Son, and of the Holy Ghost, Amen." Dean's words came out deliberately. "Bless me, Father, for I have sinned. I made my last confession just weeks ago, so I could participate in receiving Holy Communion. I wanted to be a true parishioner of St. Jude. This confession has special significance, so it will be told in a story form.

"Our story began when I knocked on the door of a local priest. I had been told that this priest would take in a homeless person. He came to his door, and without questioning me, he invited me into his home. In the weeks that followed, he opened his home and his heart to me. He encouraged me to walk with him on his daily tours of the neighborhood and county. He showed me the significance of charity, respect, and most of all, love. I cannot betray his respect or his love. He has guided my life and my soul. He asked me to become an altar boy and to serve at the daily morning Mass. I did not know what would be my course in life, but thanks to this kind priest, I now know what that will be. He would like for me to be a prize fighter much like he was in the early part of his life. True, I have enjoyed prize fighting, but it is not to be the course in my life. He must try to understand that his call has been my call. Each night when I would kneel by my bed, I would pray that God would guide me. Robert Frost once wrote in one of his favorite poems: 'the woods are dark and deep, but I have miles to go before I sleep.' If Frost was talking about the unknown and uncertain things that face all of us, and if the 'miles' are the trials and tribulations all of us will encounter, and if his 'sleep' is death, then I, also, have many things to accomplish before I sleep.

"I, too, must serve my God. I must follow His steps. If it be God's will, my life will be the religious life."

Dean heard a muffled sound. "My sin is that I failed to tell you my thoughts and my plans, and for that, I am deeply sorry."

There was a moment of silence, and then Father Dillon whispered softly, "You must know by now that you have changed my life and my dreams. For years I was just putting in my time as a priest. I was basically just treading water. I now realize that my duties as a parish priest have far reaching effects, and it was you who made me realize this. I should be the one to be thanking you for helping me to redirect my life and my duties. I was feeling sorry for what I thought were my failures. Your confession and your desire to pursue the religious life have changed all of that. I wish to thank you and bless you, my son."

Father Dillon finished his thoughts. "For your penance, I want you to say the rosary. You are also expected to honor Fitzgerald's request for a rematch." Father Dillon slowly and quietly closed the little door and left the confessional.

Dean also left the confessional. Father Dillon stood waiting for him, a wide smile on his face.

"I'm sorry, Father Dillon. I didn't want to hurt you!"

"What are you talking about, Dean? I'm getting on in age. Someone, maybe a famous young prize fighter, will be an excellent replacement. Seems to me that I know someone who fits that description. I hear that he even loves the stopping points of my daily tours."

Tears welled up in Dean's eyes. The two men, their

friendship cemented for life, walked slowly from the church to the parish house.

The old priest would have dreams that very night, but he had a feeling that his dreams would be about success, about God, and about God's love. Father Dillon, too, had finally realized that being a parish priest made him a winner also.

Printed in the United States
147098LV00001B/4/P